A PRELUDE OF PREJUDICES

Overall, I am a contemporary British Transcedentalist. A poet and priest seeking the Divine Principle within visionary authorship, as well as metaphysical arts generally. All meaning, kitchen sink drama (whether on stage, or as literature) tends to be distant from my field of interest, or for that matter, my expertise. This is not to say, of course, I cannot see any value in these stories, but rather that they need to be written without labouring points of fact everyone already knows, or adding completely unnecessary exoticisms to attract one's attention. In this regard, "sink realism" is a cultural movement whose protagonists could be described as "angry young individuals" disillusioned with society at large. And as such, the proponents of this style use techniques inherent within realism to explore complex domestic situations, which unveil controversial political and social issues; ranging from abortion, to homelessness and sexual intercourse outside wedlock. Indeed, these often harsh motifs tend to contrast sharply with the so-called "escapism" of a previous generation's "well-made plays".

That said, the writers employing these devices frequently set their stories in poorer industrial areas. A conscious methodology using the local customs and slang heard inside these regional confines to maximise their effect. Hence, John Osborne's play, Look Back in Anger (1956) is considered the first identifiable production of this type, whereas Shelagh Delaney's 1958 play, A Taste of Honey (which was later made into a film of the same name), narrates an analogously disjunctional tale wherein a teenage schoolgirl has an affair with a black sailor, gets pregnant, and then lodges with a gay male acquaintance: each part of her personal pilgrimage proving almost seminal, since issues of race, class, and gender, arise along the way. Unsurprisingly then, the conventions of this genre remain both widely attractive and current. Explaining why, perhaps, they continue to find fevered expression on British television through shows like EastEnders and Coronation Street.

So, Saule Doszhan's short story, The Tragedy of a Bastard, treads recognisable territory for us Europeans, even though the plot is placed in present-day Kazakhstan; a land faraway from our conceptual, not to mention socio-historical, spheres. Admittedly, some of Doszhan's moral assumptions read a little strangely, although the intrigues and pressures of extended familial obligation amid a family at clear war with free emotive choice, speaks volumes across our globe. Therefore, I have no hesitation in recommending this text to Anglophone readers, whilst I can only hope we see further works by this writer in future years.

David Parry
London 2018

SAULE DOSZHAN

THE TRAGEDY OF A BASTARD

London
2018

HERTFORDSHIRE PRESS

Published & Printed in UK
Hertfordshire Press Ltd © 2018
e-mail: publisher@hertfordshirepress.com
www.hertfordshirepress.com

THE TRAGEDY OF A BASTARD
&
MY OWN STRANGE HEART
by Saule Doszhan ©

English

Translated by Yelden Sarybay
Edited David Parry, Gareth Stamp, Laura Hamilton
Design by Alexandra Rey

---

*British Library Catalogue in Publication Data
A catalogue record for this book is available from the British Library
Library of Congress in Publication Data
A catalogue record for this book has been requested*

ISBN: 978-1-910886-89-2

FOREWORD

'The Tragedy of a Bastard' and 'My own Strange Heart' is a duology in which award-winning author Saule Doszhan explores aspects of the radical changes which have taken place in her native Kazakhstan in the post-Soviet era.

For centuries, Kazakhs have placed great importance on tradition and adhered to rules and values set down by their ancestors in a bygone age. Since gaining independence, the country has seen a resurgence of interest in principles and practices which are often perceived as oppressive by the current generation, leading to conflict within families and communities striving for a harmonious balance between the old and the new. In the first story, a naïve, middle-aged and highly educated woman gives birth to a child out of wedlock; an act regarded as both scandalous and selfish and which thirty years on, has a devastating effect on her long-stigmatized, illegitimate son. Doszhan sensitively portrays all sides of the situation, from the perspectives of die-hard nationalists to young, forward-looking professionals and in so doing, provides a poignant insight into both everyday life and the heritage of her country.

Her second story, inspired by Kazakhstan's first heart transplant in 2012, marks the stellar advances in medical care recently enjoyed by the country. Part fiction and part fact, it includes astonishing excerpts on the psychological impact of organ transplants and cites examples of recipients taking on the traits and characteristics of their donors.

This inevitably leads to debate concerning the ethics of transplants and whilst the medics and scientists are concerned only with the health of the donors' organs, it clearly raises issues regarding 'mixed blood' and the importance which Kazakhs have historically placed on maintaining pure lineage through generations.

The significance of the 'seven fathers' lineage' and the 'steppe passport' lies at the core of the first tale and by alluding to it again in the second, Doszhan deftly links the two to encourage the reader to contemplate how dynamically different views of the world can co-exist in the present day.

Laura Hamilton, Editor
ECG Chairman

***

'Just as Kazakhstan is emerging into a new era, so is its literature. The Tragedy of a Bastard reminds us that such transitions are rarely smooth.'

Paul Wilson, Australia

ABOUT AUTHOR

Saule Doszhan, a talented poet, and a popular writer was born on September 2, 1959 in Almaty Region.

Her poems and articles started publishing in the regional newspaper in 1974.

Her University background - the Kazakh State University "Journalism" (1987) and "Law" the Central Asian University (2006).

Being a student, she entered the collection of young poets "Audience", "Nine Keys", "Karlygash".

She gained a big experience as a reporter-journalist, editor, senior officer in the following fields: "Socialist Kazakhstan (Egemen Kazakhstan)" newspaper; the Kazakh radio;"Kazakh language and literature" newspaper; the "Ulagat" magazine; Mazhilis of the Parliament of the Republic of Kazakhstan.

A member of the Writers' Union of Kazakhstan and the Union of Journalists. A member of Eurasian Creative Guild (UK). A member of IWWG (USA)

AWARDS:

2001 - Winner of "Anuar Baizhanbayev Prize of the Union of Journalists of Kazakhstan" for the 10th anniversary of Independence.

2002 - the Grand Prix winner of the "National defender" competition, which was co-organized by the Parliament and the Ministry of Defense of the Republic of Kazakhstan.

2006 - the jubilee medal owner "10 years of the Parliament of the Republic of Kazakhstan."

2009 - the "Cultural luminary" medal owner by the Ministry of Culture.

2010 – Winner of the national contest in the genre of in the national "My country, my heart" poetry contest organized by the Nur Otan National Democratic Party.

2011 - third place winner in the "Call for Independence" National Poetry Contest.

2011 - "Honorary Citizen of Uigur district of Almaty region."

2013 – the second prize owner, the jubilee song contest "Shine, New Astana" dedicated to the 15th anniversary of Astana.

2014 – Winner, the "Military songs" competition at the radio festival with her song "March of the soldiers."

2015 – owner of the "20 years of the Assembly of People of Kazakhstan" medal.

2015 –owner of the title "Honored Worker of Kazakhstan" by the Decree of the President.

2016 – owner of the "25 years of Independence of the Republic of Kazakhstan" medal.

2016 – Winner, the "The Best Poet" nomination in the

"Independence.Literature.Writer" Forum dedicated to the 25th anniversary of Kazakhstan's independence.

2017 – Third place winner in the prose category at Open Eurasian Literature Festival & Book Forum-2017 (UK) for her nouvelle "My own strange heart."

2018 – First Prize owner in the National "The capital – bulwark of the nation" Poetry Contest dedicated to the 20th anniversary of Astana.

WORKS:

2000   "Jyr Crown" (poetry) / "Atamura" publishing house;

2006   "The secret of the third door" (prose) / Kazinform publishing house;

2008   "Baby born to the womb" (prose) / "Foliant" publishing house;

2011   "Arman kala" / (poetry) Kazygurt publishing house;

2013   "Fear in the Great House" (prose) / "Zhazushy" publishing house;

2014   "Master Almighty Pen" (prose) / "Foliant" publishing house;

2015   "My only partner" (poetry) / "Dastur" publishing house;

2015   "My own strange heart" (prose) / "Foliant" publishing house;

2016   "My own strange heart" (prose) in Russian / "Foliant" publishing house;

2017   "Sagynysh" (Prose)/ "Hertfordshire Press", London

2018   "The tragedy of a bustard" (Prose) "Hertfordshire Press", London

Author of "Maimak kaz" cartoon and about 20 songs.

THE TRAGEDY OF A BASTARD

1

"Only the Kazakhs, my dear boy, have a so-called 'steppe passport'. And apparently, you're not registered!"

Those words continued to echo in his ears as the young man slammed the door of the apartment behind him. Too impatient to wait for the elevator, he rushed towards the staircase. As he ran from the tenth floor, his feet barely touched the stone steps, often skipping them completely. Occasionally he slipped but straightening himself up, continued his vigorous descent.

The message conveyed in the recent conversation inside the apartment still made his heart pound and his breath falter and the snobbish voice of his girlfriend's father, repeated itself over and over in his head. Reaching the ground floor, he angrily kicked at the steel door. It refused to budge but the loud thud was enough to bring him to his senses and when he punched the exit button with his fist, the door swung open and he leapt outside. He emerged in an alley in front of a tall house. Finding a nearby bench, he wearily sat down but still, found no relief from the thoughts that raced through his head.

Why hadn't he anticipated that he would be interrogated with questions like this? Was he really incapable of understanding the professor's depth of knowledge and the significance he placed on such? All of this is my mother's fault, yet how can I blame such a poor soul?

He suddenly felt so depressingly lonely that a sullen emptiness overwhelmed his soul…

The girl's father, Zhetken Baquly, had not intended to pick the brains of the young man who had come to see him, but every day, his wife had nagged: "Meet him will you? The one Moldir has chosen, and give them your blessing. His relatives want to come to their engagement." So, even though it was far from customary, he agreed to meet the young man who had made eyes at his daughter. Times were changing and so were traditions. He relented and the very next day, received the tall young man who was courting his daughter Moldir. His tousled black hair and hawkish brows screamed of a strong-willed personality; an impression that was compounded by his beaming smile and his casual greeting of "Hello!" The older man was disappointed that this fellow didn't offer to shake both of his hands nor greet him with "*Assalamu Aleikum!*" in the traditional Kazakh manner. It made him think of his own students at the university, who likewise, simply said "hello". Nevertheless, having gazed for long enough at the young man, he invited him into the study.

Clearly uncomfortable, the young man pulled his legs together and sat as straight as he could, keeping his hands on his knees. Zhetken Baquly opened the conversation by introducing himself:

"I am Moldir's father. My name is Zhetken, and my father's is Baq. And what is your name?"

"Nurzhan Kalkabayev," - answered the boy, as nervous as a freshman in a lecture hall.

"So, you haven't got rid of the -*ov* and -*ev* yet?" – commented the professor, grinning faintly.

"That's what it says in my documents." – replied the boy. What else could he say?

"It's not too late to fix it. So, what type of Kazakh are you? Where are you from?"

"From around here, or the other side of the mountains."

"Are your parents there, or have they moved closer to the city?"

"I don't have a father. Only my mother. She lives in an aul[1] not far from the city." - explained the young man quietly.

"And where is your father? Where do you hail from?" – the elderly man continued to press.

Now the young man blushed and his voice grew softer.

"I don't have a father. Only my mum," - he replied.

"What do you mean you don't have a father? Are your parents divorced, or has he passed away?" – the girl's father continued his onslaught. The young man began to slouch, as if someone was pushing him down. He realized that it would be pointless trying to evade the question or try to keep anything secret from the man sitting opposite him, and in a barely audible voice, replied:

"My mother had me out of wedlock…"

Zhetken Baquly had not been prepared to hear something like this from the man who had come to ask for the hand of his only daughter. His breath faltered and his heart began to ache. For a while, he said nothing, as if he had run out of questions. The phrase "bastard child… bastard child…" crept out from somewhere in the back of his mind and began ringing in his ears. Aware that his response had come as a shock to his elder, the young man also stayed quiet. The deadly silence that descended on the room was broken only by the ticking of the clock. It was as if two people were watching each other breathing.

Moldir and her mother had left the men to speak privately, and talked in whispers as they prepared tea in the kitchen. Yet, even though her hands were busy, the girl's spirit was in the other room. Fearful of the silence behind the door, she moved a little

---

1   *Aul – a Kazakh village settlement.*

closer and listened. Suddenly, her heart leapt to her throat as soon as she heard words that could only foreshadow something bad.

"Who are these Kalkabaevs?" – asked the girl's father, breaking the silence.

"It's my mum's last name" – muttered the poor lad.

"Your mother's relatives... Uh-huh, ..."

And everything went quiet again. Both were consumed by their own thoughts. The phrase "bastard child... bastard child..." kept spiraling the brain of the old man. Even from a distance, his wife Aiganym, could sense that the conversation between her daughter's father and the young man was not going well and whispered to her daughter, who was standing by the door like a deer caught in the headlights:

"Moldir, come here and stop standing there like a spy."

And at that moment the professor's voice could be heard again:

"Nurzhan, my dear boy, there is something ambiguous about your heritage. It's far too hazy ... There are thousands of peoples in the world. But amongst those thousands, the only people who can trace their heritage through a shezhire[2] are the Kazakhs. It is true that European aristocracy and royalty kept track of their lineage, but the common folk do not know their ancestors in the same way we knew ours.

You are probably aware that a Kazakh should know his lineage through *Seven fathers*. Our ancestors marked, recognized, and distinguished their relatives through the shezhire in ancient times, when there was no written language. No other people in the world, apart from the Kazakhs, have a shezhire. Moreover, this lineage should not be tangled! For some nations, the succession of generations is through their maternal lines. But, for Kazakhs, the

2   *Paternal family tree*

bloodline runs through each father; hence the term, *Seven fathers*. Men are not allowed to marry women who share the same lineage. It is the essence of our unity that we do not marry unless we are at least seven fathers apart. This is all done to preserve the purity of the blood of our nation. After all, the future of the nation lies in the purity of future generations. This is the difference between our noble Kazakh nation and the nations that surround us. Only the Kazakhs, my dear boy, have a so-called 'steppe passport'. It can distinguish each one of us without the need for any written documentation writing and identify who belongs to which zhuz, which tribe, and which lineage. All of this goes along the male line: through the lineage of the father. So, if someone's father is unknown, then he is not registered. And, apparently, you're not registered. But perhaps your mother knows the tribe to which you belong?" – he concluded, staring pointedly at his daughter's suitor.

The young man had grown up with a scar on his heart from the fact he had always been seen as the *child of a single mother*. Thus, old wounds began to bleed again. Admittedly, since he had entered higher education in Almaty, no one had bothered him with inquiries about his origin, but now here he was, being accused by none other than the father of his beloved Moldir of having not been registered with a steppe passport. The young man froze in silence and his heart was torn with pain, as the professor continued:

"It transpires that all of our people originated from the same foothills of the same mountain. So, who could guarantee that they didn't share the same blood? However, before conception, Kazakhs have always considered the compatibility of a young couples' blood, in order to ensure the health of the next generation. There is a national sociopolitical significance in this. And even in the days before there laboratories where blood could be analyzed, the unwritten rules of the steppe served to educate its people in the principles of genealogy. So, ignorance about one's lineage, will not only cause serious harm to our traditions, but also instigate irreparable damage to the destiny of future generations. You are a doctor. You know what genetics is about."

Under the glare of the professor, the young man was ashamed and unable to utter a single word. What could he say?! The son had had to answer for his mother's mistake all of his life...

"I liked the look of you straight away, but my heart is anxious. If you don't mind, please ask your mother about your father, whoever he is. I can't give you my blessing without knowing your origins. Out of respect for the principles of our people's customs, I cannot bypass the laws of the steppe even for the man with whom my daughter is in love. None of this is the slightest, your fault and I have no right to blame you. And I would certainly never have questioned you like this, my son, had you not asked for my daughter's hand. Please don't be offended. Forgive me. Talk to your mother and come back when you know your origins."

The old man wiped the lenses of his glasses with a handkerchief, put them on and reached for a book that lay in front of him. Reading this as a signal that the conversation was over, the young man slowly rose from his seat. But as soon as he turned to go, the door opened and an elderly woman came bustling into the room, exclaiming:

"Nurzhan, my dear, won't you have some tea? At least try some bread!"

Despite her protestations, the young man hurried towards the exit and with a quick "Goodbye, agai! Thank you, apai," was gone.

Their daughter, Moldir, who had heard the entire conversation, stayed where she was, almost hidden behind the door between the kitchen and the living room. Her pale face was flushed red with shame. Desperate to leave the house in which his honour had been stained and his heart, broken, as quickly as possible, Nurzhan never stopped to consider his beloved. He didn't even stop to put on his shoes.

He just ran away…

2

Marziya lived in her father's house until her mid-thirties. She was the youngest of a family of five brothers and seemed unable to get her life in order. Her mother Aitbala, worried about her only daughter, despite considering her a sweet and balanced child; as smart as any other. Indeed, the girl who had graduated from the Pedagogical Institute, had become an accomplished and respected teacher in the aul. But still, Marziya's mother felt in her heart that being clever and well employed, was not enough to make any woman truly happy.

She was constantly grumbling at her daughters-in -law: "It's true that she is very reserved and hard for anyone to figure out what goes on in that head of hers, but even though there are five of you, no one has managed to set her up!"

The dowry, as well as furniture, bedding and kitchen utensils that had been prepared for her only daughter, remained unused and continued to gather dust. Moreover, Marziya's father had passed away with the unfulfilled dream of marrying off his daughter and meeting would-be in-laws.

The five brothers all had their own families and lived their separate lives in growing prosperity Indeed, it was only on holidays and at family celebrations, or tois, that they ever met up with and affably kissed their little sister on the forehead. She had a different relationship with each of the sisters-in-law of this ever-growing dynasty.

The oldest sister-in-law Balimsha, had joined the family when Marziya was only thirteen. Thereafter, she started calling her *little one*, and was like a second mother to the girl. The second sister-in-law was Sabyrkul, the second sister-in-law had been aptly named for she was calm and patient and as caring as an elder blood sister. Certainly, the *little one* had a lot to thank her for, and vice versa, since Marziya looked after and cared for the children of the oldest brothers until they graduated from school.

The third daughter-in-law was Turar. She was the only surviving child of a family in which her siblings had died at birth and her name meant, "the one that stays". Very spoiled and a little eccentric, she could force her husband to do whatever she pleased, and carefree, often whimsical, around his parents, she behaved as if she were their only daughter-in-law. However, she was good-natured, as well as fair in her judgement, and being a teacher, was indulged by everyone in the aul. Marziya's parents, who liked the fact that they all lived together, would not let her leave the village. She loved children and overtaking her sisters-in-law and much to her mother-in-law's delight, produced five babies in quick succession, in as many years. They were a riotous bunch but even when they turned the house upside down, leaving a mess everywhere, or fought amongst themselves, she never became riled.

The fourth daughter-in-law Zhubanysh, was regarded by Marziya as a kindred spirit with whom she could share secrets, joys and sorrows. It seems to be true that a person's name is their destiny, for the youngest daughter-in-law, Gulderai, was indeed like a flower! She was beautiful and had a flowery and joyful nature and it was as if Allah had blessed her with a life filled with pleasure and refinement. Yet she knew her own mind and contrary to Kazakh tradition that requires the youngest son and his family to live with and care for his parents, she persuaded her husband to move to Almaty. She had no intention of returning to the village and her husband's parents flatly refused to listen to their oldest son who demanded that they should either move in with their youngest son and daughter-in-law, or bring the couple back home.

"No, honey," they lamely protested, "we will not leave Kanat and Turar. Gulderai was made for the city, and besides, we'd be distracting Sanatzhan from his work"

The only bad thing about Gulderai was that she wouldn't leave Marziya alone and tracked her every move. Marziya couldn't understand why she was so competitive but even though she was the wife of her brother, the girls were of the same age, so there was more rivalry between them than kinship.

However, credit must be given to the older wives who always fussed over their only sister-in-law and were considerate of her mood from the moment they crossed the threshold of the house.

When Marziya graduated from high school and enrolled in a college in the city, she lived with her third brother Talgat and sister-in-law Zhubanysh. Until the end of the fourth year, her daily route was *home-college-home*. But then in the following autumn when she entered her fifth year, she discovered that many of the girls in her group had enjoyed summer weddings and were now married. And that was when her only close friend, Zhupar, started to open her eyes to a whole new world:

"Marziya, it appears that the two of us were so busy studying, that we missed out on a lot of the interesting things enjoyed by the girls living in the dorm. Unlike us, they lived life to the full whenever they weren't studying."

"What do you mean by that?" - asked the innocent-natured Marziya.

"It turns out that they met up with the guys from the Veterinarian Institute and Polytechnic, and spent evenings with them at the cinema or theatre."

"Oh, but who would let us go...?"

"If we keep thinking about having to ask for someone's for permission to do anything, we're likely to end up hugging only our diplomas and returning to the aul single," - retorted her girlfriend.

"Well, what are we to do? Our first priority is surely to study and gain our diplomas," - chided Marziya.

"You're right, but if we don't get married in our student years, we'll be left behind by our peers. Then back on our aul, we'll end up washing socks for some illiterate villager, milking cows, and stacking ovens."

Her friend seemed to have set herself the mission of getting married that year, and her determination began to scare Marziya.

"But how will we meet and flirt with complete strangers?"

"We need to get in touch and hang out with the girls from the dorm and tag along to wherever where the guys from sponsored institutions usually invite them. Maybe then we can hook-up with someone," - laughed Zhupar slyly.

Marziya's friend lived with her sister and brother-in-law. She didn't exactly excel in her studies, was unwilling to visit the library and what's more, regularly depended on notes made by Marziya. Indeed, coming from a poor family, she far preferred to wander the bazaars and markets with her sister.

"All right, let's go. But remember, I don't want to go anywhere with some guy like Alma's from a brick factory. And if my brother finds out, I'll be locked up at home forever." - voiced Marziya in trepidation.

Having made up their minds to become acquainted with good, educated guys with a view to meeting and marrying one that they liked, the girls started to go out.

Time passed quickly and when New Year's Eve drew near, they discovered that the guys from the Veterinarian Institute were going to invite the girls from their group to celebrate the holiday together. The news was announced by a girl named Guldariya, who had a reputation for being absent-minded:

"Girls, I've heard that Dauren's friends are super busy with the preparations and are looking forward to getting to know us." Unsurprisingly, Dauren was from a small village.

Although excited, the girls then began to fret; *what will we wear, what will I wear?* After consulting with her sister-in-law Zhubanysh, Marziya and Zhupar scoured a multitude of shops and eventually found pine-coloured dresses which would be perfect for the evening. Whilst the older sisters-in-law still considered her the *little one,* and regarded and spoiled her like a child, Zhubanysh, treated her more like a close friend. This wasn't surprising since the difference in age between them was only two or three years but Marziya, or Marzik, as she was affectionately known, cherished this friendship. Perhaps because she had grown up with brothers and was more used to boys, Marziya didn't become friends with the girls from her school, or with other girls from the institute, and as a consequence had no one but her sister-in-law with whom to share her secrets.

However, despite being the only daughter, she was never burdened with errands and since all of the household chores were largely done by her mother and sisters-in-law, she was free to spend her time reading or watching TV. Her pampered life meant that she never developed any housekeeping skills and indeed, having never so much as picked up a needle, was unable to even sew on a button.   And, although she lived in a village, she had never learned how to fire a stove, nor clean out the ashes. She had never been in a barn, let alone milked a cow! Little had changed since she had moved into her brother's new apartment in the city. She continued to be known as Marzik and continued to be pampered. Everything she needed, was handed to her on a plate and so, the thought of looking for a potential husband with whom she could set up a home of her own, never even crossed her mind.

Marziya greeted the New Year together with friends and peers in her new green dress. By attending the party, the two girls had taken their first steps towards achieving their goal and having introduced themselves to the boys danced till they dropped. They even had some wine, and both ended up walking home, hand in hand, a young man. The boy who had chosen Zhupar came to the academic building two or three days later to find her. But the guy who walked Marziya home, disappeared entirely.

"I guess my figure put him off. Look at me, I'm like a weightlifter," - she complained to her friend.

Marziya's ancestors were without question, strong, swarthy and stocky and as they say, an apple does not fall far from its tree. Hence, despite being a woman, she looked very like her brothers apart from her lighter skin and large eyes which she had inherited from her mother. Her character, according to her mother, was enigmatic. No one knew what she was thinking, or what dreams she harboured.   Until the night of the party, men had never paid her much attention, either in her native aul, or anywhere else, and she in turn, had shown no particular interest in them. It might have been that the boys from the aul were too afraid of her menacing brothers to approach her, but it also appeared that men outside, did not find her attractive. So, time went by without any sign of any suitor…

As for Zhupar, she persisted with her intention of *getting married this year* and so, was completely engrossed with in her new boyfriend. She completely forgot about Marziya who finding herself abandoned by her only friend, had no one else who could introduce her to another guy. The only men she encountered were the very mediocre, simple-minded guys from the brick factory who wolf whistled at her from across the street as she walked home, but unsurprisingly, the prospect of spending time with any of them did not suit her at all. Before she knew it, spring arrived and because she had started work on her dissertation, there was a slight change to her daily route: *home-library-institute-home.* The men she saw on public transport were always lost in thought or amidst the hustle and bustle, too distracted to give her so much as a glance, whilst those in the library, never lifted their heads from their books and papers.

Her thesis was written, and her defense was excellent. Eventually she returned to her old school when her sister-in-law Turar, a physics teacher, took maternity leave. She started work in the same year as the middle son of her brother Kanat entered first grade, and so it was she who took him to school on the first day of his classes. To have a daughter gain an academic degree and become a teacher, filled her mother with pride.

As Myrzhakip Dulatov[3]said: "*Having knowledge and transferring knowledge to others are very different things. Teaching a*

---

3   *Mirjaqip Dulatuli was a Kazakh poet, writer and one of leaders of the Kazakh nationalist Alash Orda government.*

person, that is, a child, is something of a science in itself" - meaning
that not everyone who has a diploma can be a teacher in the fullest
sense of the word. It takes real skill to teach a child. Raushan apai,
her curator at the institute, once said: "To be a teacher, you need
a heart, mind, and hands. A heart to love the children; a mind for
knowledge, and hands for skillful guidance. If you do not possess
all three, you can't be called a teacher."

Marziya always remembered these words and with due
diligence made them the basis of her work when she began - in
the words of the great Abai[4] - *to teach without sparing any effort
for the education of children.* She began her career at the age of
twenty-one and spent the next fifteen years at the same school.
But no changes occurred in her personal life.

Life for Marziya's mother Aitbalu, should have been a bed
of roses, given the attentive support of her five sons, but her
daughter's continued solitude depressed her. And for umpteen
times, she warned Marziya – "If you don't watch out, you'll be left
on the shelf! You need to build a life for yourself outside work.
Think about the future." She even prayed to the Almighty, but all
to no avail. There was still no sign of a Mr. Right on the horizon
by the time Kanat's middle son had finished school and having
completed half of his university studies, was seeking permission
from his relatives to marry. Distraught, Marziya's mother began
a new lament: "Oh, woe! Even Ruslanzhan, whose diapers you
changed, is about to start a family!"

Her brothers thought the world of her, although deep down,
they wished the only tulip among them would find her happiness.
Even though each of them had started a family and had prospered,
their hearts sank with the realization that as far as their sister's

----

4   *Abai (Ibrahim) Qunanbaiuly was a Kazakh poet, composer and
philosopher. He was also a cultural reformer drawing on European and Russian
cultural influences as a basis of enlightened Islam.*

well-being was concerned, they had met with less success.

The sisters-in-law were tired of constantly persuading her, jokingly and otherwise. Of course, they tried to find a match for Marziya - first amongst young guys, then amongst widowers and divorcees. In fact, when the wife of the deputy akim[5] of the district died, Turar found a way to introduce him and Marziya to one another. Overall, it would have been a favourable arrangement in a situation where a girl does not want to marry a poor man, but can't meet a rich one. Two children and a mother had been left in his care but Turar tried to assure her sister-in-law that this wouldn't be a problem:

- "Don't worry about the children. If you are kind to them, your husband will be grateful. You will be provided for and you can improve your life. The children will soon go on to start their own families, while this man has the whole district in his hands, and may even rise in the region."

Marziya was beginning to accept everything that she was being told, but became disillusioned as soon as she saw the groom. Allah might have given his subject a mind smart enough to govern a whole district, but had also made him short and thin. She didn't like the look, nor the voice, of this man. By this stage, Marziya was already in her mid-thirties and fast becoming a plump virgin. She felt very awkward having to sit beside such a frail candidate and afterwards, on their way home, expressed her distaste by exclaiming:

"Oh, Aunt Turash! I could have picked him up and carried him under my arm!"

Following this incident, everyone curbed their efforts; maybe because Marziya herself had cooled, or simply because the time had come for them to stop trying so hard to find a potential suitor for their sister-in-law.

---

5   *Akim – official in charge of an administrative territory*

Either way, this was the situation until seeing the psychological change in Marziya when she arrived in the city, Zhubanysh said:

"Marzik, how long are you going to continue living like this? At least have a child of your own, or something."

Over time Marziya had become an old maid. All she wanted was solitude and was reluctant to go anywhere. Her horizons were limited to treading a well beaten path: *home-work-home*. Hence, she tied the knot to her own indifference, lost interest in everything, and got quite used to a measured, monotonous life, which explained why her weight had increased with age. Indeed, it was only her pupils who brought her a sense of joy. The schoolchildren provided her with lively environment in which to work whilst the graduates kept in constant touch. In addition, she was kept entertained by both university students and graduates who returned to the aul in the holidays. They shared their latest news with her and asked for advice and some even brought her small gifts to cheer her up.

Given her long and exemplary record, she was eventually promoted to vice-principal in charge of education. A new post required greater responsibility and with that, her indifference disappeared. She became interested in life again. Keen to excel in her new role, she began to research course plans and the latest trends in teaching. Children had changed and so had their outlook on life. Their behaviour, in this era of emancipation, was also very different and in order to gain a greater understanding of the new generation and their needs, she was sent on summer courses at the Republican Institute of Education. The courses which offered an introduction to modern technologies and methodologies in education, as well as the new school programme, were attended by thirty school principals from other regions, all of whom were accommodated on campus.

This time, Marziya did not stay at her brother's, but settled in the dorm so that she was closer to her place of study. For the first time in her life, at the age of thirty-five, she decided to be independent. Up until now, she had spent her entire life obeying the bidding of her mother, brothers, and sisters-in-law and when she had studied at Almaty, had been dropped off and collected from classes by her brother or sister-in-law. As a girl, she did not go to parties or the movies, so it was little wonder that she had yet to kiss or cuddle a man; a problem made worse by the fact she was a homely girl with neither real beauty nor charm, let alone any leaning towards the type of flirtatious behaviour designed to attract men. She would speak only if spoken to and otherwise, remain as silent as a fish. Strangely, none of this had bothered her. But she had now decided to do something for herself, and when her sister-in-law inquired: "Marzik, why don't you stay with us?", she instantly replied, "Thanks! But I've my lived at home my whole life and it's time I gave the dorm a try."

"You know, you're right. Maybe it'll do you good." – laughed her sister-in-law.

"It will be. I've waited long enough. This time, I'll try to come to something," – joked Marziya.

"Hear! Hear! Let the good times roll! Maybe I'll get a fur coat for your wedding!"

Curiously, it's true what they say; crazy things can happen. A new-found sense of freedom brought unfathomable changes into the life of the old maid. She had once been told by one of her classmates, Sharaina: "When you see the one for whom you are destined, your heart will skip a beat." And that was exactly what happened the moment Marziya, who had never paid any attention to men, caught sight of Nurgali. Interestingly, he came from somewhere around Akzhaik, and was apparently the headmaster of a school. Twenty women and ten men started the courses and out of these ten men, she only had eyes for him. She saw in him a bright guiding star. It was clear from his open face that Nurgali was a good-natured man and in the breaks between classes he was always telling jokes and amusing stories and anecdotes. Furthermore, in all the schools they visited to learn about the best practices, he immediately attracted everyone's attention.

It was therefore no surprise, that   the course participants elected him as their representative. Within two or three days, he had offered to organize a getting acquainted party. Tired of dealing with family problems, endless school events, and their responsibilities to parents, and despite the reprieve offered by coming away on this course, they all welcomed his suggestion. Everyone gladly chipped in and a table was booked at a restaurant for the Friday evening.

Marziya wore a blue silk dress she had packed in her suitcase, just in case, and when Nurgali met her in front of the restaurant with a dombra in his hands, he cheerfully exclaimed:

"Oh, wow, Marziya! You are blooming today. Tonight, I'll be dancing only with you."

Having never received a compliment from any man, her face flushed with embarrassment:

"Hello?!"

"Hi! Aren't we in the same seminars?!" Approaching the girl, he wrapped an arm around her shoulder and led her into the restaurant. At the touch of the man's hands, a warm wave passed through her body, and she was grateful for his support as she struggled in her high heels to climb the stairs.

At this first meeting, Nurgali immediately realized that even though Marziya was over thirty, at heart, she was still a naive girl who did not know how to flirt with men and so, he used every opportunity to tease her and make her blush. Having initiated the party, he displayed all the skills of a good host; entertaining people with songs and playing his dombra. As promised, he invited Marziya to dance again and again.

Over the years, Marziya had attended very few parties, but even at her girlfriends' weddings, she had never flirted or danced in the embrace of a man. When Nurgali pressed her tightly to his chest, she could smell his cologne and as his hands encircled her waist as they danced, her head spun and she felt as if a fire had been ignited deep within her. And since other women were drinking without rebuttal, she too was eventually encouraged to sip from her glass of wine.

It had been a highly stimulating evening and when it was time to leave, everyone decided to head to their dorm on foot, admiring Almaty at night. Buoyed by alcohol, Nurgali joyously took the girl by the arm and from time to time, melodically called to the group to join him in song; "Friends… where are you friends?". They had all graduated in Almaty, albeit years apart, and glad to be back, walked down the street like college kids, singing songs and remembering their youth. On reaching the dorm, everyone lingered, not wanting the evening to end, and when Nurgali saw Marziya to her room, he kissed her as he wished her goodnight.

They had the following day off. Marziya spent it at her brother's, where she was casually asked by Zhubanysh:

"Marziya, you have colleagues gathered from all over Kazakhstan. Is there not a gentleman among them who is suitable for you?"

"They might have come from all parts of the country, but they are all married men."

"What's wrong with that? As they said in the old days: 'A man forty paces away from his home is single'. That's probably even more so, nowadays. Pick one that is worthy and stick to him."

"But sister, why do I need to stick to anyone?" - she blushed.

"Marziya, my dear, who else will tell you this if not me. Mum has grown old worrying about your loneliness. No matter how happy she might appear, she grieves for you. You are welcome in your house only as long as your mother is around, but you know they are waiting for their future son-in-law and the birth of new grandchildren. Everyone builds their own happiness. If you don't marry by the time colour drains from your face, you will not notice how your youth has slipped by," - she started playing the old tune.

"What colour in my face; what youth, sister? Let's admit it's too late for me to get married. Everyone my age already has families. You tried to pair me off with the widowed and divorced, but they have enough problems as it is. I don't want to deal with other people's troubles when I'm forty. I'd rather not disturb their peace," - she replied sadly.

"Then raise a child for your own comfort. That way, at least in old age, you will not be all alone. Time flies quickly; our children are about to graduate from universities."

"How can I give birth if I'm not in a relationship with anyone?" - she said softly, clearly embarrassed.

"If you don't have a relationship, then go and mingle. How long will you keep your honour as a prize?" – her sister-in-law finished with a smile.

Never had Marziya spoken so openly with Zhubanysh. She was so embarrassed she was ready to fall through the floor in shame. Illuminated by sunlight from the window, her face was flushed with fire and for a long time, she sat as silent as a grave.

Her sister-in-law placed a bowl of warm tea in front of her and then, as if driving her relation into a dead end, said:

"Listen, no matter how much you try to avoid this topic, the time has come..."

"Sister, I don't know if something will happen. But the inevitable is unavoidable..."

"I've heard that same answer for too many years. It's not something that happens by itself. Remember, the crying baby gets the milk; you've probably heard as much. Whilst you are busy with your work just now, retirement is just around the corner. When the time comes for you to claim your pension, you will be redundant. That is the law now. Unlike our grandmothers, you will not be given the opportunity to keep on working. And when you go, that's when loneliness will begin" - her sister-in-law was starting to frighten her more and more. Marziya was thinking, *how do I answer,* when her brother entered the kitchen:

"Girls, where are you?" – he called, saving her from further awkward feelings.

However, when she left her brother's house, Marziya felt so displaced from her world that she missed her stop. When she finally reached her dorm, she entered her room and throwing off her coat, fell on the bed with no desire to do anything. As she lay there with her eyes closed, Marziya's whole life passed in front of her like a movie. She had already lived through three mushels[6]. And here she was, still alone...

Apart from her brothers and mother, who was already over eighty, Marziya could see that she was alone in her heart and in her spirit. She had thought she was no worse off than other women of the same age, but they all had husbands and children.

---

6   *Mushel - twelve-year cycles measuring life.*

In contrast, Marziya spent her long days fulfilling the wishes of other people's children, aiding their upbringing, whilst wrapping her arms around her knees at night as life passed her by. She had no companion, no husband.... Her very existence felt futile and empty.

Back in her schooldays, some girls fell madly in love, received love letters, walked with guys at nights under the moonlight and sweet -talked them. Some even managed a cuddle. But Marziya did not receive any letters from anyone, and either her mean-looking brothers were to blame for this, or the boys were not satisfied with her inanimate character and unobtrusive appearance. No one confessed their love for her, nor revealed any feelings at all for that matter. And she herself did not flirt like a girl. She didn't impose herself on others. Instead, she had focused on her studies and waited for cherished things in the future. She imagined that the freedom she enjoyed in her parents' house would continue for the rest of her life.

Based on her merit, Marziya had been accepted by the institute and though hard work and perseverance, had achieved her goal and graduated with a diploma as a physics teacher. She had studied and studied, but for what? She had ended up back in her old school.

Rural guys began to eye up the girl with the teaching diploma. Yet, Marziya kept waiting for her Prince Charming, who like her mother said, would need to be some guy with a folder under his arm and a hat on his head. But he never appeared. She didn't meet anyone rich, nor acknowledge anyone poor - and time went on.

And it would keep on going. If she didn't do anything, then one day, her life would end and she'd pass away all on her own...

People around her would continue with their lives and achieve prosperity. Her brothers would weep bitterly at first, then arrange a commemoration of forty days, a year later. Her pupils would remember her at reunions but gradually, they would all start to forget her.

Sadly, she had spent her whole life following a narrow path. Perhaps she had taken too much heed to the words her mother had repeated to her from birth: "A girl should not laugh mindlessly! A girl should not leave home for no reason! A girl should not spend her leisure time with just anyone! Go to class, come home; the rest is not your business!" Curiously, she still hadn't crossed these boundaries! As soon as she finished work, she'd go to bed. Peers did not take her with them to parties, because she was always under the supervision of her strict brothers and her mother. Also, since her sister-in-law Turar was a teacher, her peers were afraid she would hear about a party from Marziya and report it to the principal. Even her closest friend Shurbankul did not tell her everything.

Who wouldn't be indifferent to everything, if they didn't communicate with anyone and used their free time only to nap? She had been below average height since childhood and a plump child at that. People were attracted by her gentle eyes but their indifferent expression was off-putting and it was this indifference that always held her back from taking even the most tentative steps, thus slowing down her already placid life. It was only now that she fully understood and realized all of this and so, she lay there, sobbingly uncontrollably, oblivious to the discomfort caused by the lumpy mattress. She lamented her senseless life; her withering youth. In the words of the poet Tursynzhan Shapai, she *grieved and cried to her heart's content.*

On Monday, the course conveners decided to take their tutees to an exemplary school in Kaskelen after class. Everyone was to taken there by bus, just like in their student years. Nurgali, as usual, was their head steward. He roll-called everyone, and the girl standing next to him marked them off on a list. Much to her surprise, whenever they got on and off the bus, Nurgali would offer Marziya his hand. At first, she felt awkward and was hesitant but gradually came to accept it since he didn't give up!

"Marziya, let's go, little sister!"

"Marziyash, give me your hand!"

During lunch he sat beside her and served her with salads and hot dishes. The girl who had never received such attention from any man, might have appeared apprehensive, but deep inside, felt secretly thrilled by the possibility that it might lead to something more...

After lunch, Nurgali sat next to her in the bus on their way back. However, this time he was silent throughout the journey and did not fuss like he had in the morning. Marziya was equally silent. Both sat quietly, as if playing a game. Sometimes potholes on the road made the bus bounce - and their knees and shoulders touched. When they got off the bus near the dorm, Nurgali announced:

"Marziya, go and get changed and I'll give you a tour of the city."

The girl who usually agreed with everything, suddenly objected:

"Oh, agai, this is my hometown, and since you come from Aktau it is I who should be showing you the city!"

"Is that so? Even better! Then you lead and your agai will follow," - he rejoiced.

Marziya did not take long to pull on some trousers and a light sleeveless top and soon emerged on the street where she was impatiently awaited by Nurgali. The girl acted so lightly it was as if she had become someone else entirely.

First, they took the cable car to the top of Koktobe, where one can see Almaty as if it were in the palm of one's hand. After a long time admiring the views of the cityscape, they had supper at sunset in the summer garden of a restaurant serving national dishes in the Medeu gorge. Nurgali sat next to the girl and holding her hand, talked about his life. The intimacy of the gesture made Marziya burn inside and feel so dizzy that she sometimes missing points of the conversation.

"Marziyash, darling, it seems that there is such a thing as love at first sight and from the moment I met you, I realized that we were destined to be together." Taken aback by her companion's open declaration, the girl found it hard to grasp whether he was speaking the truth.

"But I should also tell you that I'm not some old bachelor. I got married when I was a twenty-year-old boy, while studying at the institute. At first, my wife and I did not pay much attention to the fact we had no children. We were both students, and perhaps, in our souls, we even enjoyed the fact that there was nothing to tie us down. It felt like everything was fine and going to plan. So, after graduating, we began to work together in the same school. Being young professionals, we were immediately allocated an apartment, and it was only then that we realized that we needed a child to be happy."

When he finished speaking, he exhaled deeply, prompting Marziya to ask:

"Are you saying you have no children?"

"Yes, it's been twenty years since we got married, but we

cannot conceive a child. I thought of getting a divorce but until we met, I knew that I hadn't wanted anyone else as much as you. Maybe you are my destiny!"

This time, when he stopped speaking, he pulled her towards him and kissed her on the lips.

Marziya remembered the night when she had grieved and cried, and recalled too, Zhubanysh's advice about having a child to comfort her and look after her in the future. That said, how was it that she had met this man just when the devil was tempting her? Nevertheless, she liked everything about him and boldly pressed herself into his embrace, and despite only ever sipping the occasional glass of wine, now drank the cognac that Nurgali poured for her without any objection.

Their date in the restaurant continued in a single room of the hotel below which had been meticulously prepared in advance by Nurgali that afternoon. It was midnight, when they arrived and by then, the old maid was in such a perfect mood and state of intoxication that she didn't refuse anything. In fact, the girl showed no hesitation in removing her clothes herself, somewhat startling Nurgali, but a man is a man...

"Marziyash, dear, why didn't you say you were still a virgin?" whispered Nurgali, pressing himself repeatedly against the girl who was now bathed in a feverish glow.

Marziya usually dreaded nighttime and it took a lot of tossing and turning in bed before exhausted, she finally got to sleep. However, it was not for nothing that the poets sang: *People, speaking of the night, scold her for the pitch darkness, but they know that there is pleasure in the night*, and that night, she embraced all that it had to offer. But far from coming to this night at the behest of lust, for the first time in her life, she had fallen in love with a man with all of her heart and after melting in his arms, she lay and cried in a surge of happiness...

Nurgali had turned the girl's head with a stream of words, asserting: "I really like you. I will take you home, divorce my wife. I will be overjoyed if you give me a child." After that first night, he and Marziya lived together in her room in the dorm. Although Marziya was aware that this was wrong, she could not refuse Nurgali. Perhaps she had decided to act on the advice proffered by her sister-in-law Zhubanysh about having a child, or maybe she didn't care to think about the consequences of what she was doing. Either way, she didn't really understand why she was behaving like she was, although there might have been a subconscious thought that by becoming a mother, she could protect herself from shame and solitude...

At the end of the summer school, the participants gathered together for a farewell party, once again instigated by the ever-popular Nurgali. Everyone in the group spoke well of this skillful, handsome and good-natured man. As the old saying goes; 'If a man is praised by the people, he will definitely be interesting to women,' and this was especially true to Marziya who danced all night with Nurgali. She was naturally filled with sadness at the prospect of being parted from him in the morning but a vague sense of alarm had also sneaked into her soul. As for Nurgali, he was surprised that despite having convinced himself that he had done her a favour, the old maid, who had not allowed a man to touch her until the age of forty, had not made any demands on him. He had expected her to ask: "*Is this how it all ends? What will I do if I get pregnant? Will you come for me? Will you marry me if you divorce your wife?*" But, alas, she kept everything inside and her muteness made him uneasy.

Sometimes he regarded her with great concern in his eyes but whenever he worried about   how such a naïve girl managed to survive as a vice-principal amongst such wolfish teachers, he consoled himself with the thought that she was saved by her diligent preparation. Having to fill out of all kinds of papers is a real issue for today's teachers who in addition to working with students, are required to offer advice and submit reports to the district, region, or even the ministry. That's the thing they hated most of all - the endless paperwork – and he was relieved that in his school, they hired a diligent girl like Marziya to undertake such arduous administrative tasks.

The next day, Marziya accompanied Nurgali to his plane. He gave her his school's phone number and asked her to call him. He also promised that he would write with all his news and looked forward to receiving letters from her in return. Marziya diligently wrote down his address, along with the school and home phone numbers in her beautiful handwriting. After checking in his luggage, Nurgali then kissed her for the last time, saying:

"Don't be a stranger!"

This time, Marziya dared to let her emotions run free. She wept as she hugged him tight. He too got emotional, for after all, they had spent a whole month together and he felt sorry for a girl that was so pure:

"Don't cry, my darling! As soon as I've taken care of everything, I'll come for you from Akzhaik, like Tulegen in search of Zhibek[7]!" - he said cheerfully, hugging the girl again and kissing her cheek.

In due course, the plane took Marziya's first and only love up into the sky but little did she know that her beloved Nurgali had just flown away forever...

The school started its new academic year. Marziya rigorously

---

7   *Kazakh folklore characters, an analogy could be Odysseus and Penelope, respectively.*

got to work, sharing all that she had learned at the summer school with her colleagues. Meanwhile, she anxiously waited for word from Nurgali. Somewhere deep in her heart, a spark of hope and then anguish, kindled and flickered, then finally died. She left home early in the morning and returned after dark. She had her lunch with the children in the canteen.

"My sweet foal, you have so much work this year. Why don't you turn down the role of vice-principal? Was it not better when you just taught lessons?" – asked her mother, who made a daily habit of limping towards the door and greeting her daughter with grumbles.

Dinner was prepared by her sister-in-law Turar but Marziya was frequently too tired to sit at the table and often went straight to bed. She no longer had much of an appetite and as soon as she entered the dining room, she began to feel sick and then dizzy. "You do not eat regularly and so have ruined your stomach," warned her mother, whilst Marziya herself, put it down to excessive fatigue. Indeed, she was so exhausted by the pressures of work that she failed to notice any change in her menstrual cycle.

The next day, on her way to a school district meeting with Kunimzhan, she began to feel sick and had to stop the car twice to vomit.

"What is it? Did you eat something that was off yesterday?" – her colleague asked.

"I don't know, I just had the same as usual..."

"Have you ever had motion sickness in a car before?"

"Not that I remember," - she replied, feeling self-conscious.

Before the meeting, the two teachers headed for the nearby canteen and after washing their hands at the entrance, sat down in the middle of the room. Marziya felt fine whilst chatting to her friend but as soon as the waiter had delivered their order and wished them a pleasant meal, the smell of the food began to make her stomach churn and without having time to say anything, she jumped up and ran in the direction of the washroom.

When she returned to the table shortly afterwards, her face looked pale and having lost all her appetite, it was all she could do to sip from her bowl of tea.

"What's wrong with you; are you ill? You've grown so thin." – asked her companion. They had known each other since graduating from the institute in the same year and after embarking on their careers had become good friends. Kunimzhan who was a mother of three, yet looked like a young woman who had never given birth, had always felt sorry for Marziya's lack of a family and obvious loneliness.

A sudden thought flashed through Marziya's head like lightning: *Could it be that I'm pregnant?!* After all, she and Nurgali had shared a bed for a whole month during the summer...

"Kunim, if I ask you something, will you promise not to tell anyone?" - she ventured, as embarrassed as a little girl.

"Ask away. Although, if you put your trust in me why would I tell others?" - her girlfriend responded.

Marziya did not know where to start. How could she reveal that she thought she was pregnant? But mustering her courage and having convinced herself that, *whatever happens, I have to tell the truth to someone,* she launched forth. Because of her reclusive nature, she kept her story short. It began with:

"You know how they sent me to study in Almaty during the summer," and ended with the phrase: "I think I might be pregnant!"

Kunimzhan's good mood, after a delicious dinner, was shattered by news of her friend's secret, although she listened without interruption, to the end. Once Marziya had laid it all out, she voiced her view:

"You can get pregnant from being intimate with a man just once, never mind a month. You can also get pregnant from a rapist."

"If so, what do I do and how will I show myself to others?"- pleaded the poor girl.

"What else can you do but give birth? You're not young enough to claim you were deceived or forced into something against your will. And it's clear that you're not a loose woman. You're almost forty. Compassionate people will say you made the decision to have a child on your own and respect that, but you can't really do anything about the reaction of those who are spiteful."

Having delivered her frank opinion her friend sat quietly like a naughty child.

"But what will I say to my mother and my brothers? Poor mother, she'll probably die from all the gossip," – Marziya continued, with tears in her eyes.

"Right! That's enough talking. Since we're in the vicinity, let's go to the regional clinic and find a gynecologist to examine you."

Rising from the table, she swept her hands over her face in a gesture of prayer, and headed for the door, silently followed by Marziya.

It turned out that Kunimzhan knew a woman in the out-patients department who, having learned about the situation, led them straight to the gynecologist's office. On all of her previous visits to the clinic for her annual physical examination, and because the doctors knew she was a virgin, Marziya had always been seated on a regular chair and this was the first time she had been directed to the gynecological chair. The examination took a while, during which the doctor pressed on her stomach and jotted down some notes. He then asked:

"When was the last menstruation?"

"At the end of July."

"Could you be more specific?"

"I can't quite remember..."

"You are an educated woman and no longer a young girl. You need to take note of these things," the doctor reproached her.

Marziya, flushed with embarrassment and once dressed, was told by the gynecologist:

"You are approximately seven to eight weeks pregnant; now go for an ultrasound."

Exhausted by doubts and tired of the road, Marziya returned home when it was already dark. As usual, her mum came out hurriedly to greet her and following her daughter around the house, said:

"Thank God, are you alive and well?! You've been gone for so long."

Obviously, familiar with her daughter's demeanor; frowning and scowling with furrowed brows and not a word in response, her mother did not dare to ask anything else.

From that very day on Marziya fell into a depression. *So, this is what coming to a head means. What will I do now? What will I tell my mother?* These, and similar thoughts, did not leave her head. After some hesitation, she quietly headed to Almaty with the intention of telling her sister-in-law Zhubanysh everything. If there was one person in the world who would understand what she was going through without being judgmental, it was it was her. As for her mother, brothers and other sisters-in-law, she would wait a while longer to share what they would consider her shame.

"I did notice a change in your mood when you came by in the summer. But I thought – you're not a twenty-something. So, if you want to give birth by yourself, knock yourself out. You must now tell the man you were with. He doesn't have children, so maybe he will want to marry you," -advised her sister-in-law.

Marziya tried to reach Nurgali on the number he had given her, only to be told by the woman who answered:

"Nurgali Azibarbaevich no longer works in our school. He was transferred somewhere else."

At this, the girl fell into such a state of despair she didn't even ask, *where was he transferred to? Could you give me the phone number of his new location?*

"That's how men are! I was suspicious when I heard that he'd never called once in two months. So, he has no children? He wants to divorce his wife? It all sounds like a pack of lies to me!" - Zhubanysh uttered angrily. Once she had calmed down and before seeing Marziya off, she gave her sister-in-law what she thought was the only possible advice:

"Well, all right. There's nothing more you can do, so stop crying. I'll explain everything to mum and your brothers myself. Return to the aul and continue to work until your maternity leave."

Arriving home, Marziya tried to avoid being seen by her mother, brothers, sisters-in-law, or colleagues. No one looked suspiciously at the woman who had been full-bodied since childhood. And Kunimzhan, although they saw each other every day, did not bother her with questions. It was only Marziya herself, who noticed that the dresses she wore were becoming a little tight. It also became harder to walk and she constantly felt the need to lie down. But she did regain her appetite.

When her brother Kanat and his wife Zhubanysh came over, Marziya did not know what to do with herself. She would enter the house, then go out, and was too scared to look at her brother. In the meantime, Zhubanysh took their mother and sister-in-law Turar into a separate room and explained everything to them. Their mother began to moan and gasp when her daughter-in-law said, "The little one is pregnant."

"Oh, woe, how dishonoured we are! Oh-woe, the poor wretched soul! Has the devil beguiled her?! I was afraid she would be lonely! I thought maybe she would find, at best, some old widower. But I did not think she would disgrace herself before everyone and bring shame to her brothers," - her mother was so troubled that her blood pressure soared.

"All five of you failed to find a husband for your sister-in-law. Yet you all got married - to my sons. Could you not have given her to someone by force! My God, what will we tell her brothers?!" -cried the inconsolable, venerable old woman. Surrounded by her silent sisters-in-law, Marziya sat like a living corpse as her mother renewed her tirade:

"Hey, you dissolute girl; who is this scoundrel?"

"Zhubanysh, we've never hidden anything from each other, yet you knew about this! Find this man, if you don't want her brothers to kill her!"

"Mum, this man lives very far away on the shores of Akzhaik ... and besides, he's married…"

"At least let him take you as his second wife. Let him grow old with the one whom he disgraced; the devil."

"We can't get in touch with him..."

"Then get rid of the offspring of this runaway villain. Get an abortion. Otherwise, how will we look people in the eye? You have become a disgrace to my five priceless sons, disobedient one!" – screamed the old woman hysterically.

Aware of her mother-in-law's condition, Turar, quickly measured her blood pressure and gave her some medicine. Meanwhile, Marziya, even quieter than usual, sat in the same place like a lump of dough that had been left to ferment. Then unable to bear it any more, burst into tears and fled to her room.

Even then, the authoritative old Aitbala did not cease her haranguing:

"I hope you go blind, you worthless thing!"

Zhubanysh, as if she were to blame for everything, sat submissively before her mother-in-law, with downcast eyes. She was so dazed by the phrase, 'get an abortion!' -that she did not know how to deal with this terrible command. She realized, of course, that she had been the one who told the naive girl she should *at least give birth to a child for herself*. Now, if Marziya did not withstand the wrath of her mother and in shame, got rid of the innocent child, then the sin would fall on her! So, what did destiny have in store for her sister-in-law...?

Choosing a convenient moment after the medicine had calmed Aitbala, she hesitantly tried to resume the conversation in order to find out her final decision:

"Mum, your daughter is not twenty years old. She made a mistake, because she was too trusting. Yet, she has her whole life ahead of her. In two years, she will be forty. Other women her age already have their own daughters-in-law and are taking care of grandchildren. If we make her have an abortion in anger, then are we not to blame for her future loneliness?"

"Everything you say, of course, is true. But no matter how old she is, to have a child on the side is a disgrace to the whole family. Kazakhs call this "kurdemche" - an illegitimate, bastard child. Once, those who had anything to do with these matters answered before a court of honour and were expelled from society. In the future, when the child grows up, it will be hard for him, or her, too. It is therefore right that Marziya removes herself from this sinful business, especially being an exemplary schoolteacher and having five brothers who are all respected people. She herself grew up under a blessed shanyrak?! She offends us, the dissolute one!" The old woman began to get more and more agitated.

In truth, everything she said was fitting. These days girls set themselves the goal of being educated, become financially independent and carve out a career. They reach and grab for everything they see, while their youth trickles by. Yet when they reach a certain age, they begin to think about the future and giving birth to a child in or out of wedlock. The latter, which is on the increase, will always stand as a test of conscience and a disgrace for the family. Aitbala apai's soul burned at the thought that Marziya had joined the ranks of the latter, thereby disgracing the whole family, and placing the child at an unfair disadvantage. However, there was no turning back.

"And what shall we say to her brothers? You five are skilled operators but I am like a sorceress for whom there are no secrets. Together, we all failed to look after one girl who will now be shamed by all, including the children, when she goes to school sporting a big belly. Marziya's mother groaned loudly whilst her daughters-in-law felt hurt by her accusation that they were somehow responsible.

"Mum, my relatives live on the other side of the mountain. No one knows her there, so let's send her to them to give birth," – suggested Turar, as if she had found an original solution.

"Delightful! What is she, a girl of eighteen who can give birth and leave a child with someone else? Don't forget that she has decided to have a child specifically to avoid being lonely later in life, so how could anyone tear them apart? She will not give the child to anyone," - retorted her mother, as though she had just fully grasped the situation.

Then, still feeling personally responsible, Zhubanysh intervened, albeit without being able to offer a solution:

"Sister-in-law, mother is right. We can't take Marziya's child away. We just need to figure out what to do about her school "– she began to bite her thumb as was her habit when faced with a problem.

"Yes, of course, her condition will soon be noticed by everyone. What shall I say to my sons?" - said the mother, sighing deeply and desperately.

Having borne five sons and then becoming a respectable housewife, Aitbala lived like a queen. Whatever problems arose from relatives, they were all discussed and solutions determined within in this house and under her direction. Thanks to her five sons, her word was perceived as the law. Wherever she went, she was given a seat of honour and everyone treated her with respect. This unexpected disaster that had struck the family would reflect badly on her and result in her being seriously shamed. How could she ever look anyone in the eye? How could she ever visit her relatives? Her soul ached from these thoughts.

"Our dear ancestors said honour is more valuable than life, and they would prefer to suffer in such situations. It would be better for me to die before this becomes public!" – saying this, she dropped back on her cushioned seat.

One of the daughters-in-law ran to her with a glass of water; and another, with the blood pressure meter. "Ah, you fallen woman!" - the old lady did not stop cursing her daughter.

Though Marziya did not see what was going on, she sensed what was happening and was terribly frustrated. She wanted to go into that room and ask her mother for forgiveness, but her conscience would not allow it. So, she sat there, not knowing how to behave, or what to do. Zhubanysh then entered her room.

"Listen, it seems mother is seriously ill. Her blood pressure has soared."

"What should I do? Go to her?" - asked the girl in confusion.

"Don't even show yourself to her! If she sees you, things will only get worse. Come on, we have to think fast, then decide what to do," - she said, wiping sweat from her forehead and sitting beside her. It was obvious, however, that she, too, was not herself.

"I'll take you away tomorrow. You'll stay with us until you give birth," - she continued.

"No, the semester hasn't ended yet. I can't just quit and run away,"- Marziya muttered back.

"And what will you do now; will you stay here?" - Her sister-in-law sounded surprised. However, she did not finish by saying, *with a big belly* … the words got stuck in her throat. Looking closely, she noticed dark shadows appearing on Marziya's face.

"If I leave now, I'll be out of work and who will feed us then?" - said Marziya, starting to speak for herself and the child in the plural.

"You're right. If you don't feel uncomfortable, take your maternity leave from here. But, what will mother think of this?" – asked her sister-in-law with uncertainty, and suddenly remembering the nickname given to her mother-in-law by her relatives; *the general.*

"What can I do? I will get by. I will endure my fate. I'll stay here," – Marziya's voice shuddered and she started sobbing. The sister-in-law felt sorry for her, gave her a hug, kissed her cheek and wiped away her tears. *Well I'll be damned. The little one is all grown up*. Yet, her soul hurt to see Marziya so helpless.

"Be strong! At school, your colleagues will gossip. They may even hurt your feelings. However, you must endure! Even at home, your mum will probably frustrate you. Perhaps, your brothers will scold you as well. Yet, be patient! Nothing happens without difficulties. Your life is now intertwined with your child's," - she said, urging Marziya to be calm and self-restrained.

The middle brother, having said nothing during his stay, drove back home with his wife in the morning.

Her brother Kanat tried to avoid his sister from that day onwards. No one could say when he left the house, or when ate. It was as if he were on a long-term business trip.

Meanwhile, Marziya likewise tried not to stay at home for any length of time. She left early and came back late, and when she entered the house, she scurried to her room.

Her mother, of course, demonstrated her protest in silence: pretending not to notice her.

Only her sister-in-law Turar cared for her, always asking: "Little one, do you want to eat this, or something else? You should get some sleep."

One day, the mother couldn't stand it anymore and in private, told her daughter:

"Listen, Marziya, I carried you under my heart for nine months and nine days; raised you through sleepless nights. At least tell me the truth."

"What kind of truth do you want to hear?"– her daughter asked.

"Who is the father of the child?"

"If he comes from this aul, tell me, He'll wed you, even if I must tie him up. Maybe he's married already?"

"Mum, forgive me," - cried the sad girl. The mother's heart cringed, because her only daughter was in such a difficult situation. She could not stand it. She grabbed her daughter and began to kiss her tear-soaked face.

"Tell me who he is!" – her mother continued to ask.

"Mum, this man is not from around here, he's from far away. He has a wife, but they have had no children after twenty years of marriage."

"Let's get in touch with this unfortunate man. Let him rejoice. It would be better that you joined him wherever he is, rather than stay here to be disgrace. I'll marry you off and we'll celebrate the wedding," - said the poor mother, desperate to rid herself of the shame.

"I called him at work but he had since moved on. And he has never tried to seek me out." – replied Marziya resentfully.

"I'll tell your eldest brother; he'll find the man if he lives in this country," - her mother said firmly and resolutely.

"Mum, please don't. I can't force him to become a father for my child. This child will be mine alone. If I create inconvenience for you, I'll leave the aul,"

For the first time in her life, she was determined to follow her destiny independent of her family and her assertive tone startled her mother:

"What do you mean, leave the aul?" - she asked, suddenly frightened.

"I'll give birth and raise the child somewhere where no one knows me. And if anyone asks about its father, I will say we are divorced."

"Stop! As they say, if something drops on your head, you will bow. You're getting older and you still don't want to get married. So, raise this child. What else is there to do?" - the mother made it clear that she had to submit to her fate.

"I really hope it's a girl. When a Kazakh boy grows up, people start to ask for his surname and his family history. What's more, a girl is closer to her mother, while what becomes of a son will depend on his wife. Maybe she will not want to bother with him, but all the same she'll remind him that his mother, *found him on the road"* – Only now, did her mother begin to talk about the future fate of the child.

Marziya sat silently, as if she had lost her voice and having said everything that she wanted to say, her mother left the room.

...Marziya was filling in a school journal in a classroom when Kunimzhan came in.

"Makosh, I want to talk," - she said kindly.

"Come in, come in," - Marziya raised her head from the papers, ready to listen. Kunimzhan sat down on a chair beside her, putting her purse on the table. First, she adjusted the blue headscarf she always wore. For some reason the headscarf never stayed where it should, so she was forever fixing it.

"Have you told the principal about your situation?" - she asked, almost whispering.

"Of course not!" – grumbled Marziya. It had never occurred to her to talk to her superiors. Instead, she just tried to remain calm and kept herself to herself, whilst diligently carrying out her work. This is exactly what her friend had noticed.

"You should tell the principal. She should be made aware of the situation since she will need to find someone to replace you."

Marziya became pensive and in a trembling voice, replied:

"Okay."

The next day, Marziya sat with her head lowered in front of Hanbibi Shonaevna. When she heard about her condition, the principal was speechless. Marziya stared at the floor. Then, following a long silence, the principal said:

"Well, this is a difficult situation, Marziya Seitenkyzy. Now, because of you, the gossiping aul women will be discussing our school in a negative light. Moreover, you're not an ordinary teacher, but the vice-principal in charge of education. What will we say if they ask: *What are you teaching your high school students?* It's not for nothing that they say a fish rots from the head down." Her every word hammered a nail into Marziya's heart. As she sat with a drooping head, her tears began to spill on the floor. Noticing this, the principal continued:

"You can't save your reputation with tears. You should have thought about this earlier. You're not young enough to think you can quickly transfer to another place of work" – she understood very well that she too could not avoid reproaches. – "Now there's no way out. I can't just kick you out of school. Tomorrow, we will hold a pedagogical council. Obviously, we will choose someone else to replace you as vice-principal. You'll take regular hours before your leave" - the principal made her decision quickly.

It was as if Hanbibi Shonaevna could see the future. As soon as the pedagogical council convened, gossiping girls immediately began to seek scandal. *Why was the vice-principal replaced? How can a person let go of this position freely; especially after spending the summer doing refresher courses? Is there something wrong here?* As for Marziya, she had been plump from childhood and because she was such a quiet girl, no one ever imagined her as someone who would get pregnant out of wedlock. But then Zhanganym, a very curious woman who always knew the latest news before anyone else, and was prone to exaggeration, announced she had figured out the riddle. And she didn't just let everyone know, but decided to humiliate Marziya in front of everybody:

"Well, of course, educational work should be led by a person with impeccable behaviour. After all, how can we teach children, if we ourselves have lost our way?" – She threw her class journal onto the table with a loud thud. Everyone sitting in the staffroom looked at her, put down their papers and listened. Marziya, anticipating what she was about to say, grew nervous and wondered whether to remain seated, or leave the room. Shockingly, Zhanganym did not stop even in the presence of her colleague: the main character in her "discovery…"

"What we know today, tomorrow will be common knowledge amongst the parents. Then, having received information that everyone at this school is dishonourable, starting with its administration, a district commission will be sent for an inspection" – she carried on. The fidgety skinny young woman looked around her, as if waiting for a sign of support. Marziya sat frightened and as her knees trembled under the table, she wondered if anyone else would join the verbal assault.

Suddenly Maksut aga, sitting at a table by the window, said with disbelief:

"Hey, Zhanganym, I don't understand what you're talking about. What is it that happened in our school that could be of interest to the commission?"

"Why do you pretend not to know? Why do you think the vice-principal of education quit her position so quickly?" – the accuser was ready to lay out everything she heard then and there, before Shuak Apay rose from her seat:

"Enough! Taking advantage of the silence of others, you're ready to say god knows what. The administration decides who to promote and who to dismiss. Now let's go home, it's almost seven o'clock," Picking up her purse, she headed for the door and one by one, the other teachers followed, leaving Marziya sitting with her head buried in her papers.

From then on, as soon as chattering youngsters and the sharp-tongued women of her age came together, the conversation revolved around *the promiscuous behaviour* of the vice-principal of education. Meanwhile, Marziya's mother avoided such idle talk by telling people that her daughter would be spending the winter in the city to take advantage of all its amenities. Thus, Marziya spent the winter persevering: withstanding everything she saw and heard. But this was only the beginning of her mother's great patience for the sake of her child. As soon as she went on maternity leave, she immediately went to the city, to her sister-in-law Zhubanysh, who had urged her: *Come here to give birth. I have prepared everything.* During this particularly difficult time, when Marziya felt lonely among people; an orphan of her mother and brothers, and in short, the unhappiest woman in the world, she was shown genuine compassion by Zhubanysh.

3

In late March, she successfully gave birth to her baby boy. She had a cesarean delivery due to her considerable age and the fact that this was her first pregnancy.

In the maternity clinic, husbands visited young mothers, presented them with surprises, waited outside the windows for hours; sometimes with congratulatory posters expressing their love. At such moments, Marziya longed for Nurgali and despite everything, deep down she was grateful to the man who had made her a mother. Indeed, she dreamed and hoped: *If it's true that he has no children, he might come to greet his only one.* So, when they brought her baby to feed, she looked at him and saw his father. He had the same snub nose and thick brows...

But her soul was restless; *what should I call him,* she pondered? Who would find honour in naming an unexpected child. She would have to name him herself and fill out the necessary documents. It turned out that the birth certificate was issued in the hospital. Come to think of it, who would she sign as the father? She spent the whole night contemplating such things without a wink of sleep. She couldn't think of a surname either. *Should she write down Nurgali? Without his consent, or without a document confirming his name? Anyway, they will probably not write it down. I will call him by a name similar to his father's - Nurzhan,* she thought. However, when she shared this with Zhubanysh, her sister-in-law explained: *Without the permission of the child's father and without documents, we can't give the baby his patronymic until its father confirms him as his child. By law, single mothers give their child their own last name. In the column 'father' just put a dash. Otherwise, when your son grows up and asks about his father, what will you answer? Whose son is Nurzhan?* - thinking about this, she finally dozed off.

... Nurgali was peeking through the window. He was wearing the same blue vest that he wore in the summer. She ran to the window, happy to see him. He was silent on the other side. She, of course, was inside and kept joyfully repeating: *You have a son, you have a son!* But he was silent. No matter how hard she pulled the handle of the window to open it, to let him hear her, it did not open. Then, she decided to show him the baby, swaddling him as he lay on her bed, but when she returned with him to the window, his father was gone...

She laid the child back on the bed and ran to the window. Nurgali was walking away with his head lowered. She pounded hard on the glass, ready to break it. *Nurgali! Nurgali!* – she screamed and... woke up.

Marziya's piercing shriek made a neighbouring young woman lift her head and ask:

"What is it, Aunty?" – She had acquired this label because even though they had given birth at the same time, her neighbour was young enough to be her daughter. Marziya lowered her legs from the bed and burst into tears.

Everything happened as Zhubanysh said it would. She left the hospital with a boy she named Nurzhan Kalkabaev - who was registered with her last name. Afterwards, she was met by her brother Kanat and Zhubanysh at the exit. Her older brother congratulated her, kissed her cheek, took the child and gave it to his wife. Marziya was still uncomfortable around this brother and nearly collapsed with embarrassment.

Their mother was waiting at home. Marziya's heart began to pound and she remained standing on the threshold of the front door, refusing to take off her coat, especially, when she noticed her mother's white headscarf in the living room – a sign of anger, which could intimidate even a khan[8]. Zhubanysh, who had not told her sister-in-law that their mother was home, could nonetheless sense her mood: prompting her to say to the child wrapped in a blue blanket:

"Little one, don't be afraid, I explained everything to mother. I mean, what are we going to do? We can't leave such a precious child on the street!"

In the evening it was time to bathe the baby. Zhubanysh warmed the water, prepared the newborn's clothes, and went to

---

8   *Khan- a title of a ruler in Central Asia, much like a king.*

her mother-in-law:

"Mother, please, come and give your grandson his first bath" - she said, almost begging.

The scandalized old lady sat defiantly on an old trunk chest and remained quiet, so the daughter-in-law came closer and repeated her request.

"I heard you!" - she said sharply and disapprovingly. – "All right, I'll come over," - she continued and stood up holding her lower back.

The maternal grandmother of the child started to pray: "Bismillah, I proceed to the noble cause, not with my own hand, but with the hand of the holy spiritual guide Bibi Fatima!" and began to bathe the child. Meanwhile, Zhubanysh bustled about, running between Marziya, the child, and her mother-in-law. Filled with apprehension, she was worried that her mother-in-law might say something offensive to her daughter.

"Oh, light of my life!" - said the venerable old woman when she had finished bathing the child and passed him to her daughter-in-law,

- "You should have been a girl! Whose line you will continue when you grow up and become a man? As soon as you start talking, you will be asked about your father's fathers, and what will we answer then? When you engage a bride, you will be asked for your lineage, and what will we answer then?"

The two younger women stood silently by.

The following day, as soon as he returned from work, the brother asked his wife:

"How is our batyr[9]?"

Zhubanysh, who felt she shared the guilt of her sister-in-law all these months, was so overjoyed to hear her husband's question

---

9   *Batyr – a steppe warrior of great renown. Akin to a hero, or a* knight.

that her face immediately lit up.

"The batyr is growing, dear," – she replied.

And Marziya too, felt her heart warm from her brother's words.

"Good!" - he exclaimed happily.

Curious, to meet their cousin, the other grandchildren immediately ran to the crib as soon as returned from school.

"What's his name?" - was their first question.

"Nurzhan!" - replied Marziya.

"He's my little brother!"– said the eldest.

"He's my baby too!" – added the younger.

As the saying goes; *"A house full of kids is a bazaar"*. They couldn't have cared less if Nurzhan had a father or not. They looked with interest and endearment at the little creature and the pure love coming from these children's hearts made Marziya happy. She had given birth to her only child at the age of forty, at a stage in her life when she thought she would have no one.

The months passed and turned into years…

The noble old Aitbala felt uneasy about the fact her daughter had given birth out of wedlock and regretted that she no longer communicated with her relatives as before. The brothers were also choked with shame and did not communicate easily with other people. When the child reached kindergarten age, Marziya wanted to go back to work but instead of returning to her old school, moved to one of the auls near Almaty where living in a house which her brothers had bought her, she taught at the same school that her son attended.

One evening, at the age of five, Nurzhan ran up to her after kindergarten and said:

"Mum, Erkin says his grandfather taught him how to read their *lineage of seven fathers*. I wanted to learn it too, but he said everyone has their own grandfather who teaches his children and grandchildren. Is it true?"

Marziya flinched. She was cutting bread at a round table and distracted by this unexpected question, accidently slashed her thumb with her knife. She felt like she had cut her heart, not just her finger. Blood gushed from her hand and tears from her eyes. Seeing his mother crying and the blood pouring from her hand, the child forgot all about his question and hurried to his mother clamouring:

"Mum, mum! What happened?"

But, what could his perpetually silent, mother say?

"It's nothing, dear. I accidentally nicked my thumb. Bring me the first aid kit." Distracting her son's attention, she pointed to the shelf.

The child, for whom playing games was always more important than anything else, soon forgot his question, but his mother couldn't get it out of her head. For a long time, she tossed and turned in bed, feeling overwhelmed by worry: *Mother's words are coming true. Growing up, he will be interested in his origin, his heritage. What will I answer?* - the woman's heart was bleeding. - *Today, I was able to outwit him, but as he grows older, there will be many such questions which we will need to address in the future. I guess, we will have to face many there are still a lot of unexpected things in the future.*

Later, when Nurzhan was in first grade, he wanted his mother to help him with the homework his teacher assigned - to make a poster of his *family tree.*

"Mum, apai told us to make a family tree, with photographs of my grandfather, grandmother, father, mother, sister and brothers on it. Let's do it together. Where can I get the pictures?" – he asked as he began to lay out the papers.

"Hold on, honey. Let's find the photo album and we'll choose photos from it together,"

Marziya laid the old albums on the table whilst Nurzhan gathered together coloured pencils, glue, etc. Then, Marziya painted a poplar on a large white sheet.

"Now we'll take turns gluing photos of your relatives," - she said, and set to work. Her son was so happy sorting out photos and asking who was who.

"This is grandma!" – he cried, grabbing a photo.

"Yes, honey, that is your grandma. But first, we need to glue a photo of your grandfather; here he is, his name was Seiten. You never met him," - she cut out a small photo of her father and glued the picture to the very top of the tree.

"Now grandmother," - the child reached out.

"Next is your mother; me," - she stuck a photo in the right place and thought: *What will I say if he asks about his father?* The child remained silent, as if he knew what made his mother so uncomfortable. Three photos - grandfather, grandmother and his mum - placed in three places like the three legs of a stove.

"Now me," - said Nurzhan and pasted his photo below.

"This is a beautiful tree," – praised his mother.

"So, tomorrow I'll get an 'A', since my tree will be the most beautiful!" - the child was happy.

But nothing good happened the next day. The trouble began with the poplar.

"Mama!" - Nurzhan came home shouting.

"What's wrong, son? Is everything alright?" – his mother ran out of the back room, frightened by her son's offended voice.

"Mama! My tree was the worst," - he said almost crying.

"Why, my foal, we tried to make it pretty..."

"The other children, everyone but me, had lots of photos on

their trees. And I only had four..."

"Didn't we stick enough pictures?" - replied his mother who distracted by household chores, had failed to grasp the essence of his words.

"How? Who can I put on there? Everyone has two grandfathers and two grandmothers, their fathers, many older and younger siblings. And I have only you!" - said the son, stomping his feet.

"Why, you have uncles, cousins…" - she began.

"They are not brothers. The teacher said to paste only close relatives" he retorted. The son was still a child, but his arguments were sound and unable to respond, his mother buried herself in her chores.

"Mama!" - he called again.

"What now?!"

"Why does Erkin have two grandfathers and two grandmothers?"

"One grandfather and one grandmother from his father's side, and the other two from his mother's side."

"My grandfather and grandmother are your parents. And where are dad's?" - Marziya, sensing that her son's stream of questioning could only lead to complications decided it would be better if his attention was distracted away from such inevitable topics as: *Who is my father? Where is he?*

Being a child, he was easily steered in a different direction but Marziya was left with the lingering thought: '*Today I was able to make him forget, but he will soon be old enough to figure things out. If he then asks about his father, what will I answer?*' Frightened of speculating about the future of her son, she barely slept.

Unsurprisingly, it did not take long for the issue to re-emerge, this time when he was playing with other children from the aul on the football field. They began to ask each other about their tribes.

"Who are you?"

"Alban."

"Dulat."

"Naiman..."

Everyone apart from Nurzhan, named their ancestral tribes and when pressed by his know-it-all friend Erkin, he could only say what he knew:

"We moved here from Kegen."

"All our parents moved to this aul from elsewhere. But we're asking about your tribe?" Erkin's grandfather had clearly taught Erkin well and the boy could recite his lineage like a breeze.

"I don't know anything about it," – replied Nurzhan truthfully.

"All boys should know these things," retorted one of the gang.

"Even girls know their tribes," added a second know-it-all.

Nurzhan was at a loss, because he couldn't properly name his tribal affiliation. In fact, such questions were often asked by adults as well. He spent his summer holidays speculating about his father's relatives and his thoughts would meander towards that discourse when he was making hay and tending the sheep alongside his peers from the aul. The aksakals[10] often approached him with the question: "Whose son are you"? When one day he answered, "My mother's son", one old man even raised his voice at him: "First say your father's name!" - I have no father! - muttered the boy before being pressed – "Where is your father? Is he alive, or dead?"- I don't know. I just know that I don't have one!

"Stop it, aksakal, if he were dead, he would have said so," interjected another old man, in defense of the boy.

---

10   *Aksakal – title given to respected elderly men. Literally translated – white beards.*

"But it's a Kazakh custom to ask your acquaintance who he is and where he's from"- protested the interrogator who turning to the boy, continued – "Or are your parents divorced?"

"Stop baiting the kid," – demanded the old guardian.

Then he whispered to the questioner: "This is the bastard child of Seiten's daughter."

But Nurzhan had heard what he said. And everyone nearby heard it too. His little heart sensed that the concept of "bastard", or "koerdemshe", was not entirely good. Although he had not heard the word before, he realized it had to do with his father's absence and subconsciously seeded resentment towards him. For several days, he could not forget it. After returning home from haymaking, he didn't even attempt to ask his mother for the meaning of the word. But the phrase whispered by the old man, *bastard child* still rang in his ears and thereafter, he went out of his way to avoid situations in which anyone was likely to question him about his ancestry.

One day, when they were alone, his friend Erkin asked:

"Nurzhan, did your father leave you, or something?"

Erkin was his only friend and classmate, as well as the son of the one family in the village with whom he and his mother communicated, so he felt compelled to tell him the truth.

"Erkin, I never had a father," - he replied. The friend seemed to realize that he had asked a complicated question and decided not to say anything for a long time.

However, Erkin's grandfather had a habit of wanting to clarify everything, including the lines and heritage of the boys who gathered in the yard. He even asked to *sniff the scraps* of baby boys, to ascertain their differences from the girls. He also told age-old tales to those gathered around him on balmy summer days, of the legends and sagas of sixty batyrs from Kazakh history.

Meanwhile, while the boys were listening to the grandfather's poetic stories, Erkin's grandmother who was a wonderful woman, would serve them with broth and kurt, baursaks and butter, along with lashings of milk and tea. Nurzhan was both interested in and jealous of the happy Erkin. His mother was a doctor and his father, a teacher, and he had two younger brothers and two sisters. He loved visiting their house, where joy and merriment reigned. In contrast, when he returned from school to his own home, he would only find an eerie stillness. Mum was always in her room, and he in his, either watching TV or reading books. This grave silence was broken only by his mother's voice:

"Nurzhanchik, let's eat!"

In other words, it was a life that would make anyone sleepy. At times, he dreamed: '*I will have many children. I'll be like Erkin's dad. I'll drive them around everywhere; one to kindergarten, another to school, the third to the gym, the fourth to a study group. Mum will live with us and fry baursaks for each of us.*'

Days turned into months and months to years, and in what felt like a blink of an eye, Nurzhan came of age. That year, on his birthday, dear Uncle Kanat and Aunt Zhubanysh arrived from Almaty, along with his mother's relatives from Kegen.

"Well, let's have a look at the grown jigit!" - they said and kissed him on the forehead. It was as if Marziya had just noticed her that her son, who was taller than her, had grown up.

"My brother, Nurzhan is as tall as you," - she exclaimed happily.

A table was set up in the living room. Erkin's parents and the boy's class teacher Batim apai, along with her husband, also came to visit their neighbours.

"Now you will receive an identity card and passport as a citizen of the Republic of Kazakhstan," - the guests said, congratulating the boy and presenting him with gifts.

The next day, his mother suggested: "Let's go together to collect your documents at the registrar's office,"

But Nurzhan, who had heard that kids who had reached the age of sixteen usually went by themselves, replied:

"Mum, the other guys handle their documents themselves and I want to do the same. All I need, is for you to give me my birth certificate and to write a request for them to issue my ID card."

"Is that so?" - said mum and fell silent. Although she was glad that her son was becoming independent and knew what to do, she was worried about how he would deal with the column that referenced his father.

She was right to be worried. Nurzhan began to fill out the form given to him by the attendant of the registrar's office… and hesitated when he reached the blank space after the word *father*. What should he write? He had always known that he had no father and despite wanting to ask his mother, had never dared.

It was also a case of not wanting to hurt his poor mother's feelings, since he knew that she would give her soul for him. Up until now, everyone had just called him Kalkabaev and it had been a long time since anyone had asked; *Whose son are you?* or *to which tribe do you belong?* But none of that was relevant to the form which demanded the name of his father and the column which was left frighteningly empty, pricked at his honour. Blushing to the tips of his ears, he approached the attendant with the incomplete form and asked:

"Excuse me, can I fill this out at home and come back tomorrow?"– and having been granted permission, he dashed out of the door.

His mum wasn't at home. He dropped straight onto his bed.

His chest squeezed from the despair of being forever fatherless. Had he been a girl, he would have sobbed bitterly. But he was now a man and had always been told by his mother's relatives that, *a man should not cry; he should be a bulwark for his mother*. His classmate Daniyar didn't have a father either, but only because his parents were divorced. So, unlike Nurzhan, he knew both his father's name and those of his paternal relatives. He could recite his lineage of seven fathers without any humiliation, and his father was referenced on his passport.

At school, parents were divided into groups, according to the status of their children: Complete families, large families, single mothers, parents with adopted children, families of common-law marriage and low-income families. Nurzhan was not identified in any group, because his mother worked in the school. However, there were still those who wanted to throw it in his face. No one could sympathize with a person who always avoided places where people talked about fathers. *What kind of life is this? I'm fatherless… fatherless… fatherless. No father at all, absolutely none. He didn't divorce, didn't just leave … He simply didn't exist! How then, did my mother give birth to me, and by whom was I conceived? –*

In the end, the angry lad, unable to withstand such painful heartache, burst into tears.

His head was full of phrases from the movies he'd seen, books he had read - *a child born of an illicit love affair; born as a result of rape; born to a loose woman*. He did not want to compare his mum with these types of women and nor did he want to believe he had come into the world by any of these means. He then thought *maybe my mother adopted me?!* Throughout his boyhood, his mother had not given her son any reason for offense. She had only cherished him. Thus, even as a child and even after hurtful quarrels with other kids, he had never cried as bitterly as now.

Exhausted by his grief, he soon fell asleep and only awoke when he heard his mother call from outside his room:

"Nurzhanchik, are you home already? Come on, let's have supper..."

Nurzhan entered the kitchen to find his mother sitting in the dark but as soon as he turned on the lights, she rose with delight to greet him. However, when she noticed his reddened eyes, she asked her disgruntled son:

"What happened? Did you hand in the documents?"

"No. There is an ambiguity," –

"What kind of ambiguity?" –

His mother immediately knew that her worst fears had been realized.

"I didn't know what to write where it says *father*, so I brought the form home to ask you about it."

Marziya's heart began to pound and not knowing how to respond, she sat with her mouth shut. A long time passed without either of them saying anything and the only sound in the room was the ringing of the kettle and the clatter of teacups. Eventually, Nurzhan broke the silence:

"Mum, I'm asking you, whose name do I write where it says *father*?" – He looked straight at her, frowning deeply, as if conducting an interrogation.

"Son, you don't have a father, so you just put a dash on that line. What else can you do?" - said his mother hopelessly.

"Where is my dad? Why don't I have one? Is he a man, or a beast? Or maybe I just fell from the sky," - her son's voice grew louder. Not expecting such a furious inquisition, Marziya blushed as blood rushed in her temples.

"Of course, he's a man," - she said in a barely audible voice.

"If he's a human being, where is he? Why has he never looked for his child?"

"He does not know about you." - her voice quivered as she burst into tears. The son, understanding his mother's condition, got up and went to his room. She continued to remain seated as if tied to her chair; frozen in place. Tears flowed down her face, ripping her soul apart. She cried silently for a long time...

Three months later, Nurzhan brought home a passport with a dash in the column that said *father*. From that day on, he vowed never again, to ask his mother about his father. He was her only support, a consolation for her soul, her defender, and as such, he did not want to lay blame on his precious mother for the nature of his birth: no matter what happened.

4

In the year that Nurzhan completed his ten-year standard school, several reforms were made to the education system. Now, applicants wishing to enter higher education had to undergo standardized testing. For the first time, Marziya was convinced of the benefits of being a teacher. She prepared her son for this test throughout the whole winter and as a result, he achieved the highest scores in the region. At the time, it was considered a real victory to have a pupil from a rural school, score 118 points and generated enormous prestige for its teachers.

"Now you can choose any educational institution you like," his friends said enviously. Nurzhan did not think long. He submitted his documents to the place where he had always dreamed of going: Almaty's Medical University. He had always wanted to become a medic and indeed, when still a child, would perform operations on toy horses, cats and puppies: ripping open their stomachs. He even brought in sick puppies, cats and sparrows from the street in order to treat them. And whenever anyone was ill, he would run to help or stay by their side to comfort them. His goal was to become a surgeon and his mum was happy to support her son's choice. To celebrate his achieving the highest score and graduating from school with a gold medal, she invited her relatives to a gathering at which everyone proudly offered him their congratulations.

Although their aul was not far from Almaty, mother and son found it hard to live apart and on Saturdays after lectures, Nurzhan often caught a bus home from Sayakhat bus station to spend time with Marziya. Likewise, whenever his mother had two consecutive days off, she went to Almaty to visit him. In his first year, he started his medical training in a rural outpatient's clinic and hospital and he was so well received that the staff suggested that when he finished his studies, he returned to work there as the superintendent.

His mum was infinitely happier; pleased with her son who had matured and lived up to her expectations.

Their routine began to change break in his senior year. Nurzhan increasingly spent his weekends in the city and giving his mother various reasons, wouldn't appear at home for weeks, or even months on end. If anyone asked Marziya about her son, she would explain:

"Courses in the senior year are far more demanding and students often have internships in other cities."

But in her heart, she was concerned that her son rarely came home.

The main reason, of course, for the young man remaining in the city was his acquaintance with a beauty named Moldir. At school, his peers wrote love-letters to girls and would spend their evenings standing under their windows – instead of like him, writing up coursework and preparing for classes. Besides, because he continually felt uncomfortable that he has grown up without a father, he had got used to never revealing his feelings to anyone. Scheming girls from respectable families were only be interested in guys from wealthier families and so, paid no attention to a boy who lived with his mother in a home without any substantial income. There might have been tall, beautiful girls of a less avaricious nature who liked Nurzhan and who had graduated from school with an Altyn Belgi[11], but because of the shyness peculiar to Kazakh girls, they would never have admitted it.

His only goal in the first years at university was to study well. Since all the lectures were delivered in Russian, he also had to learn this Slavic language, and this coupled with the demands of the course, meant that he spent all his time, from dawn to dusk, studying. Hence, five days of the week flew by quickly. On the sixth day he usually hurried to his mother. Meanwhile, his uncle Kanat, reproached him at each and every meeting: 'Why did you stop visiting us a while back? Why don't you quit the dorm and live with us?' To which he replied, 'Uncle, it's more convenient for me to stay in the dormitory. The academic buildings are close by and the clinic is not far away either. They are all in the centre' –

On the day that he met Moldir, he was late for classes. As he hurried along at a jog, a girl walking in front of him dropped something. She hadn't noticed, so Nurzhan picked up the burgundy coloured, fur lined gloves which unlike the short

---

11   *Altyn Belgi – gold medal awarded to high-school graduates for outstanding academic achievement.*

mittens he had seen other girls wearing, were elbow-length. The girl walked fast and he had to rush to catch her up. Drawing near, he called out: "Lady!" whereupon, the beautiful girl in a pink top turned around and threw her long black hair over her shoulder to see who was there.

"Lady, you dropped your gloves!"

"Oh, did I? Sorry!" - she replied reaching for them.

The guy placed the gloves in her open palm.

"Thank you. How could I not have noticed?"

When the girl smiled, the world shone with her and some inexplicable feeling pierced his soul. He continued to follow the girl, who slowly walked off. He wanted to know where she was going and having completely forgotten about being late for his class, wondered whether he should walk beside her and become acquainted. Unfortunately, he didn't know any chat-up lines but nevertheless, was compelled by some unknown force to stay with her.

Nurzhan watched with delight as the girl in pink approached the medical faculty building which housed the dean's office. He was tempted to follow her when she opened the door and went inside, but stopped just in time and narrowly avoided being smacked on the nose when the door slammed behind her.

Stepping back, Nurzhan gathered himself together and as he leant against the windowsill at the end of the corridor, couldn't help but wonder about the girl: '*This means she studies here! How did I not notice her before, since we study in the same university, in same faculty? I should have paid more attention to her. She doesn't know me, and I don't know her. Maybe she's a junior student.*'

In truth, he had got to know very few people and since he was about to leave, was now unlikely to get to know any others.

Suddenly the white door opened and the girl in pink came out. Nurzhan, looked at her and started following her again. The girl with a beautiful figure gracefully descended the stairs. Having walked lithely down three floors, she headed for the large glass door. Nurzhan was at her heels. Together they went out into the street. Apparently, it was only at this moment that the girl noticed him and, smiling, asked:

"Do you study here, too?"

The guy who had followed the beautiful girl, had just got lucky.

"Yes. Unfortunately, I'm finishing this year," - the young man said quickly and happily. He felt embarrassed; as if he had committed a misdemeanor.

"Why is it unfortunate? Isn't it a good thing to finish one's studies? Whereas we still have years ahead of us," - she replied tenderly.

"By unfortunately, I meant I will not get to study at the same time as you..."

"Everyone has their time, agai!" - said the girl quickly, as if pointing to his age.

"How I would like to spend that time with you!" - blurted out Nurzhan.

"What words does Allah bestow on me," he wondered in his soul. Usually, he considered himself very abrupt. But, apparently, he had jinxed himself, because he fell silent; not knowing how to continue the conversation further. Meanwhile, it appeared that the girl was likewise surprised by his frank response and seemed too shy to say anything else. However, Nurzhan came up with something:

"Your agai's name is Nurzhan!" - he said and extended his broad palm to the girl. Interestingly, she didn't give herself airs as some do, but introduced herself by holding out a small hand:

"Moldir!"

The guy, gently holding the girl's fingers, laughed good-naturedly:

"Thank you!"

"Thank you, too!" - said the girl, beaming.

Their relationships after this encounter, continued as friendship. Love came to them gradually, quietly and imperceptibly. All in all, Nurzhan was pleased that he had become close to Moldir - not through his friends, or accidentally, like in movies and novels, but through the feelings they experienced for each other. Indeed, he felt like a happy hero in a wonderful narrative. In the mornings, he awoke full of joy and flew to his classes as if he had wings. After classes, he would wait for the girl named Moldir in front of the academic building, in a state of blissful anticipation. He used to run to Sayahat every Saturday, hurrying to the bus to see his mother, but now everything had turned upside down and instead, it was Moldir whom he hurried to meet.

Moldir was a tall girl and, even though she looked quite imposing, she was really as naive as a child. She had liked Nurzhan at first sight, perhaps because he was a little older, and quickly became very attached to him.

They spent that autumn together and then the winter, which they found strangely favourable despite the harsh weather. And then spring came, renewing everything in the world: awakening all of nature, breathing life into the living. Spring also marked the beginning of a livelier existence and perhaps inevitably, awakened stronger feelings between Nurzhan and Moldir. They realized that they wanted to place their trust in fate and spend the rest of their lives together and began to think about ways they could approach their families and receive their blessing.

The also had to consider the fact that after graduation, Nurzhan would be allocated a post elsewhere:

"Moldir, we will soon be sent to different places according to our specializations. Obviously, they will not let me stay in Almaty. In my first year, I was assigned to the Semipalatinsk region, where there are not enough doctors, and I will surely be sent there again."

"What should I do?" - the girl was sad for a moment.

"You will continue your studies here. If we get hitched before the summer, we will enter into a legal marriage and then the administrators must take into consideration that my wife is a student and allocate me to Almaty. We have this as a possibility," - he replied.

The girl, who was a third year, hadn't been thinking about getting married just yet. But she didn't want to let her lover go to the ends of the earth alone. However, it was clear that both her father and her brothers would not agree to an unexpected marriage. So, the girl was caught in a crossfire. The upheaval in her soul, left her silent and confused.

Each of them was consciously aware of this and sat quiet for a long time. Yet he was still a man. Hence, Nurzhan was the first to make a decision:

"Moldir, I'll talk to my mother. We must get married," - he said firmly. Then, considering it inappropriate to sit silently, the girl hesitantly said:

"My family will probably not agree, I'm still in my third year."

"Don't worry; I'll get to know your parents. I will explain the situation to them," - he soothed, accustomed to solving all of life's issues himself. But he didn't say was that he *would speak to his mother on the same subject.*

"You'll do what? You'll startle my father. He strongly adheres to Kazakh customs. What will he think if you come to him?" - she answered. Alarmed by the thought, she sprang from her seat.

"Are you that afraid of your father?" - asked the young man, for whom her father's influence was not entirely clear.

"Of course! We're all afraid of him. Neither mother, nor my brothers nor the daughters-in-law decide anything without father. In our family, his word is the law and not subject to discussion."

"Then, it's difficult. Maybe if your mother took your side?" - he said, remembering that his mother defended him in any situation; always supporting him.

"No! Mum would never do that. On the contrary, she's always saying things like: *Father is coming, get ready! What if he hears this! If dad doesn't approve, it won't happen! Father's word is final! Father's opinion in this family is the law!* That's how our mother brought us up. Even my brothers, with their own families, don't do anything without dad's approval. And the daughters-in-law do not enter into conversation with our father."

"By the way, do your sisters-in-law greet the elders in their husbands' family with a bow?" - Nurzhan became interested.

"Not only my sisters-in-law, but mother herself still welcomes our brothers and daughters-in-law this way."

"Why does she do that? She is the elder" - Nurzhan asked, since he had never seen his mother bowing to anyone else.

"Kazakh women greet this way, to ensure that their husbands will enjoy good health, while they also ask forgiveness from God on their behalf," explained Moldir. "My mother was raised in Kazakh customs and adheres to them."

"And you'll likewise welcome our daughters-in-law like that?"

"Of course! And your uncles and aunts and the eldest in the

village. Mum has taught me that this form of greeting is a sign of courtesy."

"If you meet the elders in our hospital, will you greet them like that, in your doctor's robes?" - laughed Nurzhan.

"What's wrong with that? Of course, I will! Where we meet is where I greet them. Even in lab robes. If I wear a mask on my face, then I'll take it off and greet them," - the girl smiled tenderly.

"That's my clever girl!" - Nurzhan drew his beloved to his chest and kissed her forehead. Moldir immediately quoted the lines of the poet Kadyr:

The Kazakhs did not kiss girls,
Never hurt girls or their honour.
Only hugging them by their waist,
Sniffing their foreheads instead.

5

When her son told her that he wanted to introduce Moldir to her future mother-in-law, Marziya was put in such disarray that she headed for Almaty on the earliest intercity bus. First, she went to Zhubanysh to whom she described in detail her son's love and how she had come to meet this girl. Marziya was usually so laconic that her tone surprised the sister-in-law:

"I'm so happy for you. If you want, I'll come with you to meet them" Having agreed to this suggestion, the pair set off but, on the way, Zhubanysh stopped and said:

"Little one, it is important that you get acquainted but it would have been better to invite them home!"

No wonder it is said that good ideas often come too late and this explains why these women came to their senses and abandoned their trip. Marziya liked the idea and exclaimed:

"Yes, you're right. I'll let Nurzhan know that he should bring Moldir to our home. As they say, better late than never. Now, it's late, but it's good we remembered the correct way of doing things." Marziya, who was in a rush to see her son and his fiancée the expression, joy and fear go hand in hand, was partly elucidated the dazed women's return home and the fact they bought all types of delicacies at a store along the way.

Not long afterwards, the doorbell rang and graceful but coy girl crossed over the threshold. The arrival of such a courteous, admirable girl on Nurzhan's arm instantly filled the house with joy. Marziya and Zhubanysh ran around preparing the table, glad that Kanat and the children were not home to interrupt them. At first, they didn't know where to place the future daughter-in-law but eventually decided that Nurzhan and Moldir should sit at the head of a large table in the hall. Seeing the girl hesitate, Zhubanysh gently urged her to take the seat of honour:

"Daughter, today you are our guest; please be seated. The time will come when you will sit lower and pour tea" – and with these words, she led the young woman by the hand to the feast. Obviously excited, the women rose to the occasion by constantly fussing about. Marziya poured tea, while her sister-in-law served hot kuyrdak. Nurzhan was likewise dizzy with happiness, albeit rather overwhelmed by the fact he had introduced this beautiful woman to his two 'mothers'. Meanwhile, Moldir, blushing to her ears, kept her eyes lowered as she sipped from her bowl of tea and ate her food.

After a while, Zhubanysh told her nephew:

"Nurik, you go to the kids' room. We girls must have our

secrets!" However, despite the fact that she was happy to look at her future daughter-in-law, Marziya had no idea what to say to her. As for Zhubanysh, she was an experienced mother-in-law who already had two daughters-in-law, and so ignoring the girl's shyness, took the initiative to open the conversation. Through a series of questions, she managed to acquire everything she wanted to know about her nephew's intended and once satisfied, said to Modir: "Let's go to Nurzhan. I will introduce you to our children, even if it's just by photos" – As she left the room with the girl, she quietly gave Marziya the thumbs up and whispered:

"Little one, your daughter-in-law is perfect, so tell your son not to lose her."

When she returned, Marziya was sitting smiling and looking dumbfounded.

"Are you just going to sit there smiling? You must meet the in-laws as soon as possible. Don't worry about the wedding; you have five brothers, as well as five sisters-in-law and none of us will be lazy when it comes to organizing the celebrations." Zhubanysh was so excited, one would have thought the wedding was the very next day.

"Nurzhanchik said he would first get acquainted with her parents and they would set the time for a visit," answered Marziya, who would never initiate any business of this sort without consulting her son.

"Then make him hurry! Marry your son off this summer. Otherwise, he will be allocated a hospital at the other end of the world," - pressed the sister-in-law, scaring Marziya.

From that day onwards, Marziya did not leave her son in peace but he too, was keen to make the acquaintance of the girl's parents as soon as possible, and soon afterwards, announced:

"Mum, I have decided that this Saturday I will go to Moldir

and meet her parents." In a state of agitation, the mother set out her son's finest clothes and once he was dressed, led him to the morning bus and prayed to God that He would send him good luck.

The following Saturday, Nurzhan arrived home on the last bus. Mum waited impatiently in the courtyard and seeing her son's silhouette, joyfully ran to the gate. But as he drew close, she saw that her son looked despondent and was clearly in no mood to talk. A troubling thought flashed through her head: *Did they really reject him?!*

"Nurzhanchik, I thought you were coming tomorrow," – she exclaimed, pretending not to notice her son's gloomy demeanor.

"Well, I've come, now haven't I? How are you?" – replied her son as he entered the house.

Hardly daring to step over the threshold, Marziya thought: *'My God, what happened to him?* Instead of following him inside, she busied herself with some petty chores in the yard, but since it was already growing dark, she couldn't stay out for long. Eventually she entered the house. Although Nurzhan was in his room, the light was off and when she looked inside, she saw her son lying on his bed fully clothed.

The sense that something was very wrong, filled her with alarm and unable to bear it any longer, she called out:

"Nurzhanchik, get up. The soup is ready. Won't you have some?"

"No, I don't want to eat,"

His apparent lack of appetite set off alarm bells and his mother's heart began to pound; *something bad has happened.*

Suddenly, the bed springs creaked and sitting up, her son announced: "Mum, we need to talk!"

His mother entered and after turning on the light, crouched

in front of him. He remained quiet for a while and then angrily
burst out:

"Moldir's father said I should learn about my origin."

At these words, Marziya's heart plummeted. She would have
preferred to die than hear this. Her carnal pleasure, experienced
over a month with Nurgali, had become a punishment for her
only son. Indeed, even when he was in the womb, he had been a
reason for ridicule, gibes and gossip: a kind of thorn in her side.
She had given birth to her son to offer her consolation in this life.
Her intentions had been true yet he became the target of slander
by enemies and mockery by friends. It was as if his very existence
had ignited fires of human anger. From the day he was born, she
had adjusted herself to the attitudes of everyone around her. If she
heard something mean, she pretended not to hear it and did all
she could to shield her son from such things. But it now appeared
that there was nowhere for either of them to hide from the truth.
What would happen now...?

She remained kneeling, lost for words.

But Nurzhan started demanding answers:

"Mum, I'm speaking to you. Will you finally lay out the
whole truth about my conception?"

"*My God, what should I do?! What shall I say!*" – Marziya's
voice screamed in her head. "*No, I owe him he truth!* ... Having
resolved to do what was right, she raised her eyes to gaze at her
son. Dying from shame and seeing her whole life flash before her
eyes, she told her son everything.

"So, now we can find my father and talk with him?" - asked
Nurzhan, as if looking for a way out of an impasse.

"Before I gave birth to you, I called him. His colleagues said
he had transferred to another school. I was confused and didn't

even ask where he was transferred to."

"Do you know what tribe he belongs to?"

"At that time, very few people were interested in Zhuz, or a person's affiliation. It was fashionable to just use the playful phrase - "My address is the Soviet Union". He is most likely from the Younger Zhuz; probably an Adai."

Again, Nurzhan was silent for a while:

"Mum, you need to tell this story to Moldir's parents,"- replied her son, seeing no other way out.

"I'll go if they want to hear me out," – agreed his poor mother. Of course, she would do anything for the sake of her child. She was even ready to face her future in-laws and despite her shame, try to sort things out.

A week later, Marziya decided to meet with Zhetken Baquly's wife. She wanted to take Zhubanysh with her, but her son was against it.

"Mum, it's not right to enter into such a delicate business with someone else present. Go by yourself and tell her all your secrets," - was his advice.

And her son was right. First, she would explain the situation to the girl's mother; then see what happened. So, on the agreed day, she left on the morning bus. Nurzhan met his mother at the Sayakhat bus station and they immediately headed to Moldir's house.

He pressed the apartment's bell and told her:

"Mum, you go now."

"And you… how will I…?" - she did not have time to object. The locks of the door were opening.

"I can't!" - said the son and fled down the steps. At that moment, a door opened and a woman in a white kerchief appeared.

"Hello, I'm Nurzhan's mother," - said Marziya.

"Hello... Come on in, welcome" – Moldir's mother offered her light slippers and they went into the living room.

The house was silent.

"Make yourself comfortable. My husband is at work. The sons have their own houses. Moldir is at her lectures," - said the venerable woman, to allay her guest's fears.

Marziya sat down on a soft sofa and looked around. Old furniture! There was no blatant display of wealth that would immediately catch one's eye. Everything was just right; modest, simple.

"Let's have some tea and make our acquaintance," – offered the woman and removed the white cloth from the table in the middle of the room. The table was covered with all sorts of delicious food.

The hostess then brought a large white samovar:

"You can rinse your hands; there on the right," - she pointed to the bathroom.

"Now let's get acquainted. My name is Kerbez. I'm Moldir's mother. Her father's name is Zhetken. She has three brothers and three sisters-in-law. She is our only daughter and the youngest of our children," – chatted the woman, placing a bowl of tea before her guest.

"My name is Marziya. Nurzhan is my only son. He has no father..."

After this, the women talked for a long time and muttered together about the vicissitudes of fate. Kerbez, understanding the situation, said:

"Now we need to convey this to her father."

"Let me tell him, when we meet," – began Marziya.

"No! We have a different way. We can't just tell this man

everything directly to his face. I will first consult with my sons and they will tell their father," -the girl's mother fussed.

"Well, all right. Whatever you decide," - said Marziya, embarrassed by her words.

"Good. We'll get in touch," – finished Kerbez, opening the door. When Marziya took the elevator downstairs and went out into the street, her son ran up to her. Of course, he had waited and worried for a long time. So, he immediately asked:

"Well, Mum?!"

Sitting on a bench in the alley in front of the house, Marziya told her son exactly what had happened. When they reached Sayahat, it was already dark, but Marziya managed to catch the last departing bus.

Nobody could change Nurzhan's allocation to Semipalatinsk. Furthermore, following the revelations of Marziya to Moldir's mother, there was still no news from the family and his mother was very worried. *How can this professorial family give their daughter to a fatherless son of a single mother? Of course, we are not their equals, which means Moldir's love for my son wasn't real. She learned about our poverty and turned away from my son,* Marziya thought bitterly. However, she did not talk about any of this with her son.

And the son could not tell his mother he had already met with the girl, or that she couldn't do anything without the blessing of her father, stating,

"I must at least reach the senior course; otherwise my father and brothers will not give their permission."

When he suggested to Moldir: "What if I kidnap you?" - the girl got really scared.

"Are you mad, Nurzhan? My elder brother is the deputy

head of the city's department of internal affairs. With his help, my father would immediately track us down and take me home,"

"In that case, it's unlikely that I can never win your hand," – replied Nurzhan sadly.

"My dear, be patient for just one more year. As my mother is fond of saying; even the skin of a hare can last for a year." – At this, she tenderly clung to him and continued, - "then my studies will have come to an end".

When they had strolled long enough, Moldir asked:

"Why are you so gloomy?"

"How can I be happy when the moon in the sky is closer to me than you? It is everywhere in front of me, whilst from tomorrow onwards, it will probably be impossible for me to see you," - replied Nurzhan.

The next day, Marziya and Moldir saw Nurzhan to the east-bound train. Embracing and kissing his mother's cheek, he jokingly said his farewells: "Mum, if you can still wait another year, I will make Moldir your daughter-in-law, even if I have to steal her. As long as we're alive, time will fly. The main thing is that Moldir keeps her promise," – Filled with hope, the young doctor set out to start a new life in a new land.

As the surgeon specially allocated to their regional health centre, he was given a cordial welcome by his new colleagues and even received a personal welcome from the head of the regional health department.

"Welcome, Nurzhan Kalkabayuly!" – greeted his boss. The patronymic *Kalkabayuly* sounded strange to the young man, since no one had ever called him by his first name and patronymic before. Yet sitting before the leading figure in his new world, he didn't think it appropriate to point out the error by saying, *this name is not my father's, but belongs to a relative of my mother.* If he had, then he would naturally have been asked whose son he was…

From that moment on he became Nurzhan Kalkabayuly. The head of the department showed the young specialist around the facilities and promised to provide him with everything he needed, including an apartment for the rest of the year. As if all the people of Semipalatinsk had been waiting for surgeon Kalkabaev to arrive, he was inundated with patients all day long requiring either routine or emergency operations. The latter were brought in by an ambulance, so when he came to work early in the morning, he did not notice how many had arrived the previous evening. It was only at nighttime, when he returned to his dorm, that he remembered his mother and his beloved but he was often so tired that he could feel himself falling asleep when he talked to them on the phone. Yes, there was considerable distance between him and Moldir, but their hearts still beat in unison. They understood each other without words. Sometimes, both would silently hold their phones for a long time, only listening to the each other's breathing...

And his mother endlessly rejoiced at his words:

"Mum, if they allocate me an apartment before the New Year, I will transport you here myself!"

To Moldir he would also say, only half in jest:

"I'll get an apartment. First, I'll bring my mother, then I'll kidnap you!"

"I miss you!" - she answered.

But the head's promise of an apartment was delayed.

Unlike Almaty, the winter was long and severe and beset with snowstorms. The frosty cold air often left people, including Nurzhan, feeling breathless but warmed by the attention of the people at the hospital he barely noticed the whims of the weather; nor the passage of time. Eventually, since the apartment did not work out, he couldn't let his mother move in and nor did he visit Moldir for he was as restricted in his movement as a horse on a tight rein.

With the spring came the long-awaited news; like a crack in the permafrost. Nurzhan received the keys to a two-room apartment in a new micro district. However, the heating was inadequate and since there were other structural faults, he spent most of his spare time refurbishing and refining his digs. How could he ever expect his mother to live in such a place and indeed, negotiate the mudslides whenever she left the apartment? So, he decided to wait until the earth dried up. Before he knew it, summer had come. He had such a longing for Moldir that he sometimes felt he couldn't do anything and work became difficult. When he heard her voice on the phone, he became so excited that he wanted to drop everything and fly to Almaty. But, if he did go, wouldn't it be in vain?! After all, she would just repeat her excuse: *Father will not let me go*! And as soon as he thought: *has the girl turned away from me?* - his heart turned cold. He himself was true to his word, although when it came to Moldir he was helpless. Therefore, he kept quiet: unable to tell her the sharpness he felt.

The summer came,
And our lands blossomed.
So why have you changed,
Teasing maiden? -

The young man often sang this popular song, when thinking about her and missing her. In the end, he could stand it no longer and having excused himself from work for a week, flew to Almaty. Moldir met him herself, and when she clung tightly to him, their young souls, their fervent feelings, seemed to be in seventh heaven. *We will never part now!* - he thought.

But it didn't work out.

The professor did not budge from his principles. So, convinced he would not be able to marry Moldir that summer and having to leave her with tears in her eyes, Nurzhan travelled back feeling very depressed.

There was one however, one positive outcome from his trip: his mum, who had retired by that time, agreed to go to live with him, while the weather was still warm. Although Marziya did not want to upset her son, she decided to express her opinion this time:

"My dear, if it were not for my original mistake, then you would not have lost your way in life and would not have lost your happiness. Not everyone marries for love; there are other girls besides Moldir. Any of them will happily marry you. What is more, the people here seem to be good. Think about it!" - she said.

"Mum, only Moldir will be my wife! If she does not change her mind, I'll never change mine! I need someone like Moldir, who loves her nation, who respects her father and husband: a girl brought up by her mother. If my father and mother betrayed the rules of our people, I won't. Moldir's father explained to me our noble national virtues. Now, we need to protect and continue them. In truth, only then will our offspring be pure. I am convinced it depends on each of us whether the nation will be healthy or not!" - he declared as if opening his mother's eyes and waking her into consciousness.

Ready to sacrifice herself for her son, his mother, having moved to Semipalatinsk, began to get used to snow blizzards and frosts in this region.

6

Moldir graduated to the final course.

Her mother, Kerbez, did not like the fact that her daughter had become a house dove. When she came home from university, she would immediately sit down in front of her computer.

She recalled how she had upset her father two or three years ago by deciding to marry the son of a single mother. She remembered how his mother had frankly confessed to everything and then tearfully asked her not to blame her soul, -

"Don't let my burdensome fate be a hindrance to the love of our children. I was not some street girl who didn't know the father of my child. I gave birth to him when I was a mature adult and could distinguish the good from the bad. My son's father was also of good standing. So, there will not be any incompatible mixing of blood: even his zhuz is different. He hails from the vicinity of the distant Ural Mountains; a place so remote that even birds, let alone galloping horses can't travel anywhere in a single journey. Would you pass this on, to your husband please? Let him give his blessing. As soon as we hear from you, we will send an intermediary."

This request of the boy's mother was not a burden on the heart. She mentioned every detail to her husband who after hearing her story, told her: "Karbez, let's end this conversation. My daughter is still young. Let her at least finish her studies."

No one dared to contradict the head of the house, so they did not debate his decision. Despite understanding her daughter's feelings and no matter how sorry she felt for the young man, the mother could not go against her husband and therefore had had to tell Marziya:

"Moldir-zhan, told the young man her father still hadn't given his consent. Moreover, he had said she should finish her studies,"

What could an unhappy daughter do in such a situation? She went on a hunger strike: closing herself in her room and cried all day. The next day she went to classes with swollen eyes, and became self-absorbed from that moment onwards.

Nurzhan made a point of attending the celebrations following Moldir's graduation ceremony. His goal was to talk with her father again and to then send an intermediary for matchmaking. Obviously, the girl was shining with joy having finished six years of hard study and receiving a red diploma. Arriving home, she first showed her father the precious red cover - the result of her many years of toil.

"Yes, you can be proud of this! And now here's a gift from me and your mother!" He returned the diploma with an enclosed envelope and kissed his daughter on the forehead. Her mum, also kissing her, added:

"Your brothers have also prepared a small iron mustang for you."

Moldir and Nurzhan had come to the same decision: They would ask for her father's permission together. She was exhausted thinking about what to say and was banking on her mother's support. They both knew that it was time for him to make a final decision as well as show leniency towards Nurzhan, the man who for years, had been patiently waiting in the wings for her:

"Dad, I have a request of you."

"Speak, today you are the winner. Today is your day!" The

father took off his glasses and listened attentively.

"Dad, Mum, I beg you, please hear Nurzhan again!" – the girl blushed with embarrassment.

"And who is he?" – asked her father, who had either forgotten, or pretended not to remember. Obviously, her mother knew and looked wide-eyed at her daughter.

"The guy who came to you. I have finished my studies, while he has waited all this time," - the daughter continued in a trembling voice.

"Ah, that guy?! Is he still following you around? I've already told him that I did not have a daughter who would follow a man without a past," - her father retorted sharply. He made to get up and leave, but for some reason, sat down again.

"Daddy, his mother came and told you everything; did she not?"

"My dear, one cannot correct a mistake with words. It is everyone's duty not to make such mistakes." - having spoken, he looked at his wife, as if blaming her for all of this, and then looking at their daughter, asked in a slightly gentler voice:

"Where is this guy? What is he up to now?"

Feeling sorry for her daughter, the mother joined their conversation:

"After finishing his studies, he was sent to Semipalatinsk. He was given an apartment and took his mother into his house."

"What did he study?"

"It turns out he's a surgeon. He's been working there for three years and was recently appointed chief physician of the city hospital."

"How do you know all this?" – replied the man irritably, whilst casting an angry look at his wife. – "Well, well" he added as if to himself, "so he ended up in the cold!" He then marched off to his study.

According to the rules of the house, no one entered that room without reason. So, both the daughter and mother stayed quiet. Meanwhile, Moldir understood from her father's conversation that he did not like Nurzhan, and began to try persuading her mother:

"Mum, is Nurzhan guilty of the fact his father left them? How long must we adhere to our traditions; the laws of the Steppe. It's not the nineteenth, but the twenty-first century."

"Moldir, respecting the customs of our ancestors has nothing to do with do with what century we're living in. They are passed from generation to generation, from century to century, so that the health of our nation can continue to improve. And to keep uphold those customs is the duty of each of us."

"Some know about this, others do not. If anyone asks, we could just say that they are divorced," – snapped her daughter.

"Okay, we can hide from people, but we can't hide from Allah. Who knows what lies ahead. We see how in neighbouring countries people marry relatives, mixing blood. You yourself are a doctor and he's a doctor and so you know the outcome better than I do," – persisted her mother, unprepared to back down.

"Mum, we are not related. He is from the Younger Zhuz, whilst I am from the Senior Zhuz. That's it; I'll run away with him," - the girl said, stomping her foot.

Kerbez, who had never seen such behaviour from her daughter, grew afraid: *If she runs away with this scoundrel, her father will kill me!*

"Moldir, talk to the older sisters-in-law. Let your brothers persuade their father, if there's no other guy in the whole world for you!" - And with that, she stomped off into the kitchen.

This time, Moldir did not cry. She had already tried crying and even starving herself, but no one listened. *All that's left is to run away,* she thought, as she recalled how Nurzha had cradled hope under a boulder of despair whilst waiting for her over a thousand kilometres away, ready to give his soul for his beloved. She had lost all sense of peace and couldn't sleep, and then without a moment's hesitation, decided to go to her youngest sister-in-law. She was kind woman who was always with her in both sorrow and joy, and when they met, she cheerfully cried:

"Molly, your brothers and I were going to congratulate you tomorrow on your diploma. But since you're here, come on in! The brothers have a very beautiful gift for you," -and let slip what should have been a surprise.

However, the girl, whose head was spinning, told her everything; beginning with the love she felt for Nurzhan stretching through the years and ending with the disagreement between herself and her parents. She also mentioned that the young man was in the city and if possible, they wanted to get married that year. Finally, her relative agreed to help:

"Yes, your situation gives rise to a big problem. I'll talk to everyone in advance and try to explain things to them. After that, we'll all go together to express our concerns to your parents," – She then treated the sister-in-law to a kuyrdak and gave her tea.

Moldir's soul was filled with joy by the conversation, and she immediately told Nurzhan, who had delayed his return to Semipalatinsk whilst waiting to hear from her. Encouraged that the end was in sight, they celebrated by going to the cinema and afterwards, supper in a cafe.

Eventually, the whole family of Zhetken Baquly gathered to

celebrate his daughter's higher medical education diploma and presented her with a small Korean car. Apparently, the sisters-in-law had already had a good discussion beforehand, so after the feast, veered the conversation towards the girl's future plans. The talk touched on her relationship with Nurzhan but when the elder sister-in-law Gulnar was about to report they wanted to send matchmakers, the father-in-law raised his hand and said:

"Dear Gulnar, as far as I'm concerned, that subject was closed three years ago."

The daughter-in-law, who never contradicted him and never crossed his path, bit her tongue. Moldir's heart sank and her eyes glistened with tears. Noticing this, the younger brother interjected:

"Dad, let the young man come. Let's get acquainted!"

"I can see the guy is good, and understand that his heritage is not clear! I also know that we cannot change the principles that have been passed down by our ancestors over the centuries, but surely... we must accept Moldir's choice. It's she who will be spending the rest of her life with him, not us."

At this, the older brother rejoined: "Father, there is truth in what my brother has said but Nurzhan's origins must be worthy. We need to set an example for people in the future. We can't send my sister away with just anyone!" – It appeared that he was taking his father's side.

The sisters-in-law began to whisper among themselves. The aksakal's wife, Kerbez, watched him. Then, the head of the family, seated in the place of honour, cleared his throat and asked for his children's attention. Everyone exchanged glances as they waited to hear what he had to say:

"I have never interfered in the private lives of my children," - said Zhetken Baquly, - "I always thought, they have their own heads and they know what to do. However, Moldir has stepped away from the path of her ancestors and so I have choice but to rein her back." His angry words were like a scourge that whipped Moldir and she leapt up and fled to her room.

The happiness of the occasion was completely ruined. Hence, the daughters-in-law, excusing themselves to the father, gathered the dishes and were ready to retreat to the kitchen when they heard their father's menacing cry:

"Sit down!"

All three of them immediately obeyed. In the sudden silence, they could all hear the girl crying in the next room. But choosing to ignore this plaintive sound, the head of the family embarked on his lecture:

"Let me make something clear to all of you! Over the centuries, the human race has been struggling with its history. In Europe, aristocrats and kings have their genealogy, but their common folk did not know their ancestors.

Yet, throughout time, whenever they communicate with one another, Kazakhs have always asked: *What is your origin? Who are your ancestors? What zhuz are you from? Where are you from? What tribe do you belong to? Who was your grandfather? Do you know your roots?* Kazakhs, therefore, delved into the important aspects of the family trees or "shezhire", of whoever they met. In modern terms from the point of view of genetics, they recognized and clarified this historical data. After the excursion through the "Shezhire" they even proceeded to establish the following:

1. The person's origin;

2. The compatibility of their offspring;

3. Their four related lines: their father's lineage, their father's mother's relatives, and relatives from the wife's side.

I did not invent all this; this is the PRINCIPLE of the

whole people. It is an unwritten law, passed from generation to generation and chronicled by Tohtar Abyz. In the Soviet era, Kazakhs were unlucky enough to lose their identity. However, thanks be to God, our history is now being restored and people are returning to their true religion: Islam," After taking a sip of tea from his bowl, he continued in a calm voice to tell everyone about all the events that had taken place since Nurzhan visited him:

"Nurzhan's mother, it turns out, was a teacher. She did not fall into her situation because she is a loose woman. Yet, even if our family understands and accepts this, what about the order of our ancestors who for centuries paid special attention to our people's dignity? Our people have long suffered hardships and misfortunes and it continues to be our duty to maintain our national traits: to keep up with civilization whilst passing those spiritual values that have preserved national consciousness to the next generation. Overall, our ancestors honoured the shezhire to preserve health and ethnic quality. They adhered to an important goal - to continue the family in a legitimate, dignified, pure manner. In which case, those who committed actions that are alien to our religion and national consciousness were expelled from society. Those born as a result of debauchery or out of wedlock were even buried separately, and any bastard child labelled a "kurdemche", and isolated from everyone. In troubled times, they were neither mustered nor listed. It was said: *He who does not know his lineage for seven fathers is not well-born.* This is why our ancestors attached importance to propagation and received their blessing from generations of married people. With the concept of a sacred hearth, our offspring continued in legitimate marriage. Knowing all this, how can I as an aksakal, give my daughter and her suitor my blessing just because they love each other? And just because we're living in a different era? If every father was faithful to the principles of his ancestors, and every mother brought up her daughters to give birth in the accepted manner, there would be no bastard children stigmatized for being without kith or kin!" – The old man was getting more and more heated and could barely contain himself. Nobody interrupted his lengthy speech. Knowing that everything he said was appropriate and intelligible to the heart, each member of the family listened in silence. But Bolat, who was the youngest son in the family and used to speaking freely, commented:

"Father, everything you say is true. We must preserve national customs and traditions. But the deceived mother of Nurzhan did not abandon her child as is the way of many modern women."

Taking advantage of the moment, Kerbez sided with her son and in support of her daughter crying in another room, added:

"Indeed, she raised and brought him up well."

"There are many such situations among people, but that doesn't mean that we should allow it to afflict our family." Once again, the eldest son spoke out in defense of his father.

The father sat and watched his children as if he had just challenged them; *now, try to refute my words:*

"Whenever this appears amongst our people, it must be cut to the roots to prevent it spreading any further!" - he said and ran his hands over his face.

"It is now the twenty -first century. Some thirty years have passed since Nurzhan's birth and in that time, his mother has more than made up for her youthful mistake by raising her son well. So, why should she carry any blame?" The youngest son would not let up.

"Father says we need to keep the family tree to the seventh tribe; adhere to the principle of observing healthy offspring. You only have to look at the sick children in our society to see the results of intermarriage between relatives. These problems persist despite our laws that prohibit incest." The eldest son continued to push his original line.

"Dad, in my opinion, there is no problem of mixed blood in this instance because Nurzhan's mother knows that his father is from the shores of the Urals. It is clear that his heritage is far removed from ours, and so the principle of our ancestors would be preserved." The middle son now entered into the debate.

"Well, let's say you are right, but what about the legality of marriage? Why should we ignore that issue?" - the head of the family inquired, looking around him with eyes bulging.

"Father, we're on the threshold of the twenty-first century! Other nations, are embracing globalization and if we are not careful, we will remain a static nation, entrapped by tradition and forever looking backwards instead of to the future." The younger son was growing increasingly frustrated.

"Hey, son! Are you aware that in the world's most developed nation and today, in the twenty-first century, the Japanese remain wholly committed to the preservation of their ancient traditions and such is their respect for the elderly, that they carry their parents on their backs?! One hundred percent of them speak their native language, in addition to many having five other international languages. There is also no divorce!" - his father retorted angrily.

"Father, please calm down!" – begged their mother.

"Dad, if the unhappy girl is not allowed to enter marriage legally, what will she do? It's not like in the old days, when girls could be forced into marriage without their consent. Do you really want her to face a life alone without a husband or children?!" Implored the youngest son.

"Father, there is truth in Bolat's words too. There are many lonely old maids nowadays. You know, our friends have three daughters living in their father's house; the oldest is about fifty. This is a disease of modern society" - Kerbez supported her younger son.

"So, what if she doesn't get married? Will she produce illegitimate children? What will be their fate? Or is a child a toy that everyone who's afraid of loneliness can make for themselves?" – said the aksakal looking menacingly at his wife. The senior daughter-in-law, for fear of ugly complications in the conversation, then announced:

"Zhamilyash! Let's warm up the tea!"

"Oh, it's gone cold. Warm it up, dear," – agreed her mother-in-law.

"And in the meantime, we'll stretch our legs." The eldest son stood up from the table.

The eldest sister-in-law entered Moldir's room to find the girl still lying on her bed, sobbing.

"My soul, I understand your position. Let father calm down, then we'll talk again" – she said, hugging her through the blanket.

"My father will not rest. It's now been four years, and he's still angry," - Moldir replied through hiccups.

"The brothers will continue talking to him," - the sister-in-law added.

"If he does not agree, I'll run away! I've already been allocated to Astana," - the girl said, continuing to sob.

"Are you really going to go to that cold land?"

"I'll leave. It's the new capital, the city of youth. The future is there! I'll start a new life with Nurzhan in a new environment!" - The girl sat up, raising her head.

"Let's go, we brought some hot dishes," - the middle daughter-in-law called everyone to the table.

The younger son, trying to force a decision during their earlier conversation, said:

"Dad, excuse me if I said too much. I'm going to talk to Nurzhan myself! He has suffered from childhood, grew up without a father and endured life's adversity. However, for so many years he waited for his beloved, as befits a true and honorable man. I support him."

The brothers sat silently, not knowing whether to reject, or support, his bold proposal. The old man, realizing that the children were waiting for his decision exclaimed:

"My children, you probably think I am an old man who has been hardened by age!" - he looked around, as if he were in an auditorium. – "or do you think I'm a soulless father, blocking his only daughter's road to happiness?" - he raised his voice.

"Father, please, how could we think that?" - the oldest son fidgeted.

"I'm a person who adheres to the traditions of our ancestors. And your mother is the same. I think other parents who consider themselves Kazakhs adhere to them as well. Therefore, being devoted to these very traditions, while having grown fond of a legitimate wife, I raised such sons and a daughter as you. As my offspring, it is your duty to continue my ways. Yes, now is a different time. There are new laws and regulations. You marry the ones you love and those who fulfill your desires. Yet, the duty of parents is to give their children direction, so that when they fulfill these desires they must adhere to the customs of our ancestors and not go beyond them. Yes, there is not a person who doesn't make mistakes, who doesn't lose their heads. *The good ones are not those that don't make mistakes, but the ones who correct their mistakes* – however, these words of our ancestors are not appropriate in this case. Conscious of all this, how can I give my daughter my blessing? When I die, you must also make such a strict, but fair, objective verdict in similar situations; even if it is difficult. Only then, will the souls of our ancestors be satisfied!" - he finished his speech.

The children, realizing the aksakal would never give his consent, stopped the conversation. So, the evening of the celebration of the diploma, ended sadly. When the brothers left, the mother entered her daughter's room.

"I have been sentenced. Have you come to tell me that I should happily accept it?" - said the daughter, taking a deep breath.

"Stop it! What sentence? Hope dies last! He will calm down," - she began, but her daughter intercepted her:

"He will not calm down! I know it! I'm leaving for Astana! I'll spend the rest of my life alone!" - she declared.

"Oh, darling, you are throwing me between two fires!" – replied her mother, who now feeling completely feeble, literally collapsed on her daughter's bed.

"Mama! Mama!" - exclaimed Moldir, holding her mother's head. – "What's wrong?"

"I think my blood pressure has risen and my head is spinning," – gasped her mother. She was overcome with the unbearable grief that her only daughter, the apple of her eye, had in the words of Abai, experienced the biggest disappointment in life at its very beginning...!

7

She loved her parents, but having failed to persuade them to give their consent, Moldir left for Astana on a beautiful day in August. When the plane eventually, landed at the airport of the capital. Nurzhan, was there to meet her and holding hands, they went straight to the City Department of Health. After their meeting, the head of the department, Mazhit Shaidarov, a tall man with a trimmed moustache, asked:

"Are you husband and wife?"

"Not yet ... I'm in charge of a city hospital in Semipalatinsk, so living in different cities, we can't marry," - answered Nurzhan half-jokingly.

Seeing how well they suited each other, the satisfied Mazhit Zeinululy then asked:

"What is your main specialty?"

"I'm a neurosurgeon."

"Oh, as it happens, I've just heard there's a vacancy at the neurosurgical centre, so it sounds as if I should send both of you there so that you can start working together!" The head of the department firmly shook hands with the man, as if giving him a blessing to start his new life ...

MY OWN STRANGE HEART

Novel

The creation of the story is connected to the latest achievements
of the national medical sciences

Dear Reader!

The unique heart transplantation surgery conducted in August 2012 in the National Scientific Cardiosurgical Center of Astana was the reason for writing the story "My own strange heart." Its successful completion is certainly a national achievement, a testament to the fact that the medicine of our country has risen to the world level. This news amicably pleased everyone who heard about it, and, as an indicator of our healthcare, increased confidence in it.

There is nothing more valuable than health and life itself for people. As a result of my writing effort and inspiration, this essay is dedicated to the doctors with gifted hands.

It seemed to me that if I write this story simply as a fictional read, I will not be able to properly inform my reader about the successes of our healthcare. Therefore, I decided to insert, in italics, all the newest medical achievements in the narration. I ask to excuse me in advance if I inadvertently made a mistake in some terms or scientific concepts in my work.

Accept this truthful narrative as a labor born of immense gratitude to people in white coats and patriotic pride for the achievements of our national healthcare.

Sincerely,
Saule DOSZHAN.

I

- If only I survive... If only I survive... only survive... only survive... survive... surv...

Whispered young man quietly, connected by a tube to the anesthesia apparatus through the throat, but soon his mind blanked out and he lapsed into oblivion.

What will he do if he stays alive?! Will he be able to move mountains if he survives? What dream was in the heart of the fellow, who will undergo heart replacement, when he fell asleep on the surgical table under the anesthesia. Will he wake up?!

And then the sliding doors of the third operating room noiselessly opened...

In a spacious and cool room, the four walls of which are coated with steel, two operating lamps hang from above, whose bright light seemingly increases the contours of all objects.

There is an operating table is in the middle. At the front of the table is the monitor – and the main life-supporting device. It records electrocardiogram (ECG), shows heart rhythms, blood pressure, and oxygen content on it. A mini laboratory for the analysis of blood drops is in the far corner of the room. It is designed for immediate blood analysis in any required quantity.

On the other side, there is an artificial electric cardiac pacemaker that monitors the rhythm of the heart.

In the table latches there are needles, sets and other things necessary for surgery.

To the left of the operating table, a TV is mounted under the ceiling to monitor the surgeon's work.

All this is the newest, the most modern equipment used in world medicine. In the room, depending on the complexity of the surgery, there are two cardiosurgeons, one perfusionist, one anesthesiologist, two nurse anesthetists and assistants.

Near the operating table, the anesthesiologist and assistant set up a breathing bag in the anesthesia apparatus.

The assistants get dressed, cover the surgical area with sterile sheets. The room is absolutely clean.

Doctors have a belief, "The surgery will go the way you prepare for it." Therefore, every surgery is prepared extremely carefully, scrupulously. The intubation process is especially important for them. *This means preparing the patient for surgery.* They get everything ready for timely injection of blood and medicinal preparations into the blood vessels. The second surgeon prepares the main patient: he opens thoracic cavity for surgery.

A surgeon does not perform any surgery alone, let alone a heart transplant, and even regular coronary artery bypass graft is carried out by a whole team: two operating surgeons, two specialists providing artificial blood circulation, two anesthesiologists, blood transfusion specialist, and nurses. When all these specialists work as one, you can hope for a successful surgical result. Conducting a surgery is similar to the performance of a grand opera work by a group of musicians. Everything should start with one note and end in one breath. After this, the patient is transferred to the resuscitation department...

And this surgery was a very unusual one. No one can guarantee its successful completion. The patient, who for a long time was thinking about whether or not to go for the surgery, knows this himself. Perhaps, the fact that Yuri Vladimirovich did not disguise anything from the patient served its purpose. So, it was with this patient, the surgeon honestly said, "the surgery is very complicated. So far, such surgeries have not been conducted in Kazakhstan. At the same time," – he added, "there is no need to be afraid too much, everything will be fine."

At this point, the two main heroes – cardiac surgeon Yuri Vladimirovich Pya and his colleague Jan Pirk, who came from the Czech Republic, carefully washed their hands, baring their to elbows in the next room. They are dressed in flax cotton suits of green color. Both wear optical glasses, which increase the objects tenfold and emit light.

Everything is agreed in advance, because both specialists are calm and silent. The day before, a large detailed meeting was held with all participants of this historic work. All unforeseen circumstances that could arise during the surgery were scrupulously discussed. Now, it seemed nothing else was left except for the surgery itself.

From the bottle tap that hung on the wall they again applied antiseptic on hands and with arms outstretched forwards both surgeons like wonderworkers entered the operating room.

The assistant served aseptic napkins. Wiped hands pulled on rubber gloves. The assistants put robes on the surgeons and masks on their ears. It turns out that the chief surgeon ties the gown belt himself only. It is also a kind of insurance against infection.

At this moment, the most sacred of the saints for this moment – the HEART – was brought into the room in a special container...

Both brigades started to work.

Assistant-helper began to cut the skin with an electric knife.

The smell of burnt skin filled the room.

Electric saw cut thirty centimeters of chest bone.

In the open chest cavity, the sick heart of the man appeared.

Yuri Vladimirovich, like a musician pressing the keys of the instrument, quickly began to operate his fingers on the coagulator buttons.

Competition with nature began...

Began!

It is for the first time in Kazakhstan that the heart replacement surgery began. The National Scientific Cardiological Center in Astana is one of the best medical institutions in Central Asia. To save the life of thirty-eight-year-

old man Zhanibek Ospanov, who has suffered from unstable angina (angina pectoris) for a long time, a risky attempt was made to transplant, implant the donor's heart.

For countries with advanced medical technology, replacement of organs is not a special wonder. Citizens calmly change sick organs, take medications and keep on living as if nothing happened. As the world media reported, four years ago, a thirty-three-year-old woman who underwent heart transplantation at the Jerusalem hospital Adasa Ar-a-Zofim, safely gave birth to twins. In Western Europe and the United States, skilled in advanced technologies, replacement of human organs is seen as ordinary, everyday procedure. And what do we have?

Today there are many people in our country suffering from heart and liver diseases, thousands of patients need kidneys replacement. Besides, how many babies are born with a sick heart! Eighty percent of babies with congenital heart defects die before they reach the age of one. This is one of the most sensitive issues on the agenda for a small country like Kazakhstan, which population barely reached 17 million people. All these categories of patients are now queued for transplantation. However, we must admit that a person who is in such a queue, if a donor will not be found, will live at best one to two years.

Number of citizens suffering from cardiovascular diseases is not decreasing, even the tendency of growth is observed. People began to understand that in the case when medications do not help, only organ transplantation can. The number of young people under the age of thirty who need immediate transplantation has increased. The poor people, suffering from pain, desperately rush to various instances. They communicate with foreign clinics through the Internet. When it comes to such surgeries, foreign experts are overexploited with appetites.

And abroad, huge funds go only for surgery. And after all, a lot of money is needed to cover travel and food expenses. And where a sick person can take such funds? They begin to look for sponsors, and they are difficult to find in our time. Relatives begin to rush around, tell everyone about their problems, but, alas, they do not dare. Meanwhile, time is lost. Every day and every hour they work at the cost of health. The patient, lost hope, falls into despair and slowly fades away. Once a spark of hope completely fades away...

In order to support this spark of hope, domestic medicine is looking for all possible ways. As of today, only 25-30 percent of transplantation are solved from the point of view of medicine in our country, the rest, as it turns out, bump into the issues of legislation, human sanity and religious concepts.

All this depends not only on the knowledge and competence of doctors. First of all, relevant material base and large funds are needed here. Besides, before the completion of such a step, the readiness of the society itself is of great importance. For example, using heart, kidneys, liver and other organs of a person died in a traffic accident, many sick people could be saved from impending death. Of course, this requires the consent of relatives. And this should be stipulated in a special law.

Kazakhstan has solved this problem.

Probably, not everyone knows that the Code on Health of the People and the Healthcare System, adopted in our country in 2009, provides for legal norms on transplantation. The 169th article of the Code reads, "Recovery of tissues and (or) organs (parts of organs) from a corpse shall not be allowed if the health organization at the moment of removal was informed that during the life this person or spouse, relatives or legal representatives have declared their disagreement with the removal of tissues and (or) organs (parts of organs) after death for transplantation to the recipient." If a person during his life did not say anything about removal or non-removal of organs, relatives also did not speak on this matter, in accordance with this article, based on the "presumption of consent," an organ is allowed for removal from the corpse.

Members of the Parliament after a long discussion in 2009 introduced relevant norms on transplantation in the law. They say that the body of a deceased person can be withdrawn after the death of brain, and if the person suddenly died, withdrawal is permitted with the consent of relatives. Thanks to this, a small but possible transplantation of heart, kidney and liver has appeared. However, it is not yet possible to say that these norms of the law work completely.

In accordance with the Governmental decree "On the establishment of a departmental working group for development of regulatory and legal acts on the development of the organ transplantology sphere," a working group was formed, and this case has somewhat moved now. Let's hope that additional norms concerning the issues of transplantation and organ donation will be introduced into laws and regulatory acts.

Medical specialists improve their qualifications abroad, pass internship in the CIS countries, in particular, in Belarus and Ukraine. As a result, A.Syzganov National Scientific and Surgical Center in Almaty has already managed to transplant heart and liver successfully for the first time in the country. Only kidney transplant was practiced in the country before this. And heart transplantation is not one of those things that can be treated in a disorderly manner, out of hand. That is why, no matter how the doctor improved qualifications, the issue of heart transplantation should be treated according to the principle "measure thrice and cut once"...

*Transplantation is transplantation of one person's organs (kidney, heart, lungs, liver, etc.) or tissues of one part of the body to another person. In medicine, the giver is called **the donor**, and the taker, that is, the patient – **the recipient**. In general, it should be noted that in Kazakhstan organ transplant surgeries have already been conducted for more than 30 years. There are people among us, who having given one kidney or part of the liver, saved lives of others. But especially necessary organs for needy patients can be taken from deceased people. Head of the Bureau for Coordination of Transplantation Karashash Abauova said in her interview to journalist Aigul Seilova, "A number of important measures are held at the National Medical Holding Centers of Kazakhstan in order to develop organ donation and transplantation. Highly specialized transplantation assistance to the population is provided free of charge at the expense of the republican budget. Along with this, it should be noted that transplantology is not similar to any medical system. With the joint participation of citizens and medical workers, organ transplant surgeries will become available to the people. In our country, relatives of "potential donors" in many cases for various reasons do not give permission for removal of body parts of the deceased for trans-*

plantation. They are just not morally ready for this. Therefore, relying on for-
eign experience, when it comes to transplantation (after death), every person
should express own opinion on this issue even during life."

"I think," Karashash Abauova continued, "since our body lives belongs
to us in our lifetime, we ourselves must make decision whether to give or
not to give someone our organs. This information should be kept in a special
state information system. Only certain specialists should have access to it .
Along with this, the republican information base of patients needing organ
transplantation should be compiled. This is a big and necessary thing. For
example, for today in our country transplantation is made in seven clinics.
Each clinic has its own list of patients who need organ transplantation. For
constant and proper monitoring of condition of such patients, it would be
good to make a single system of such accounting. In this case, it would be easy
to compare the blood group, weight of donors and recipients, compatibility
of their tissues and other parameters. I believe that all these problems will
be solved by the Republican Center for Coordination of Transplantation,
created at the National Scientific Medical Center."

The society on proposals of the World Health Organization should pro-
vide itself with donor organs. The lack of donor organs is felt everywhere.
This is also peculiar to the most developed countries. First of all, organ trans-
plants are performed for the residents of the country, i.e. citizens of own
country. After that, opportunities are being thought through on how to help
others. Therefore, our countrymen who wish to undergo surgery abroad, are
waiting for the turn for transplantation for years. Currently, more than 100
patients are on the waiting lists of the Ministry of Health for foreign surger-
ies. The youngest of them is two years old.

Severely ill people expect only good from society. They all want to live,
look to the future with hope. And heart replacement surgeries are made at
the expense of the state budget.

In our country, the issue of the sale of organs has not yet been raised.
The lack of donors primarily hampers achievement of this goal, improvement
of heart and liver transplantation. In a word, there are a lot of problems.

The word "dono" in Latin translation gives the concept of "I present,
I donate." I think only very kind people can become donors. For this, they

must have perfect consciousness and high human concepts. Unfortunately, there are no people who respect those who live after them and are ready to sacrifice their organs for that. In our country, donor organs are mainly taken from people who died in a traffic accident or from another disaster, people who are in the state of death or suddenly died. Even in these cases permission from the dying person or relatives is needed. Such circumstances complicate the problem, precious time for patient is lost.

In this regard, Serikzhan Yenshibaiuly, specialist of the Shari'a elucidation unit of the Spiritual Directorate of Muslims of Kazakhstan, said in a conversation with the media, "Transplantation of one person's organ to another is allowed while observing the following conditions of Islamic Sharia. First, the necessary organ only is removed from the deceased person. A person is considered deceased when the heart and the brain stop working. Secondly, in Islam, the sale and purchase of parts of the human body is not allowed. Only before death, he must bequeath his organ to another person, leave the order. And with sudden death, this is done only by permission of close relatives. Thirdly, before the removal of the body, it is necessary to have a medical opinion that this body will really benefit another person. And if the organ is removed from a living person (if he gives a kidney to his relative) this should not damage his health. It is considered unrighteous to steal and sell parts of the human body, which are now being talked about in society. Fourth, organ transplants should take place only in case of emergency. It is allowed only when medical preparations do not help anymore, the only way to save a person is to replace the organ. This requires professional opinions of specialists. Fifth, consent of the person taking the organ is needed. All that has been said is the conclusion of the scholar theologists, adopted at a special world conference. I would like to say one more thing, there is a notion that on the Judgment Day every organ will answer for a person. When transplanting, the organ will answer for the person to whom it was transplanted.

Recently, from the television broadcast I learned that we have a lot of donors. It turns out, in addition to those who died in accidents, there are so-called "unwanted" people who do not have relatives. However, no matter how unwanted he was, it is forbidden to take organs. Our Prophet (s.a.a.w.) said, "The infliction of harm to the deceased (breaking his bones) is equated to harming a living person." Therefore, taking advantage of the fact that the person is dead and has no close people, it is not allowed to remove organs, use or sell them. In general, the removal of organs is not forbidden, but the consent of a person is needed."

From this statement one can understand from where Kazakh society got the concept that dismemberment of the body of the deceased person, transfer of organs to another person contradicts the mentality and faith. They say, who hides the disease is doomed. It is because of this reason today we lag behind the world development trends, it is also an obstacle in resolving this issue.

I think everyone understands that the thoughts of doctors involved in transplantations are pure. The great goal is the preservation of human life. The conclusion is that in our country, a new medical way of preserving human life has just started to be applied.

The National Scientific Cardiosurgical Center successfully carried out the replacement of the heart – the most perfect type of transplantation – doing it for the first time!

In the course of the surgery, the specialists of the Republican Scientific Center of Emergency Medical Assistance and the Republican Diagnostic Center made all possible assistance.

The man who was on the verge of life and death was successfully implanted with a donor heart and it immediately started beating: beat... beat... beat... In unison, the hearts of the members of the team that successfully performed the unique surgery were happily beating.

The man, who in anesthesia oblivion was raving, "if only I survive!", after a six-hour surgery survived. The new heart awakened him with rhythmical jolts, as if announcing that great things are ahead of him, a long life awaits...

II

In the ears of the man, who was lying in the center of the reanimation ward on the bed with a snow-white sheet, connected by various tubes to the medical device, from afar, a voice called him, "Zhanibek! Zhanibek!" A weak voice was heard, but there was no strength to answer.

His head is heavy. He wants to open his eyes, but his eyelashes seem stuck together. Teeth, as if crammed, tightly squeeze the endotrialchial tube, inserted into the mouth. Dry lips do not unclench. Some subconscious feels that he is breathing through his nose.

Where am I? I had a surgery planned for yesterday. I'm alive, so the surgery was successful... Consciousness again became clouded.

It is not known how much time passed, consciousness again returned to him. He made an effort to open his eyes, stirred his eyelashes. He tried to lift the cast-iron head, but barely moved it.

" Awoke! Awoke! "– the muffled voice of a nurse, who was sitting near to him, was heard from a distance.

Someone, stroking his forehead, said, "Zhanibek!" He realized that this was his name, he tried to respond, but because of the tube in his mouth he could not move his lips. He had no voice. He made an effort to open his eyes. Eyelashes slightly disjoined. He felt the tender touch of light.

"He opened his eyes!" – someone exclaimed joyfully.

Where does he lie? Whose voice was that? Isn't it Munira's voice? Failing to say something, he fell asleep again.

So, between life and death in a deep sleep, under the rhythmic beat of a new heart, Zhanibek spent another day.

Through the window of the adjoining room, the duty doctor and the nurse one by one followed his condition not getting a wink of sleep. Cardiosurgeons Yuri Vladimirovich and Makhabbat Sansyzbaikyzy came two or three times, listened to heartbeats and checked the body temperature.

One can say that from yesterday every second of Zhanibek Ospanov's life was under the control of not only this center, but also the entire republic.

The surgery was successfully completed.

The donor heart did not feel like a stranger in the new chest, beating confidently and rhythmically.

The recipient who received the organ, underwent a six-hour surgery, recovered from anesthesia and began to show signs of life.

The human heart by its every beat reminds of a pump, which ensures delivery of blood to the furthest point of the body. With each beat, blood is accelerated by vessels with a certain force. This force is called blood pressure. The heart works without stops and for a day forces blood make up to a thousand turns in the body. It has a special property to work all life without stops and rest. As scientists say, this is the only motor in the world that works with no stops.

As if confirming the research of scientists, the new heart was beating steadily, and the pressure was, so to say, 'like astronauts have'.

The surgery made to Zhanibek Ospanov, in its importance can be compared to the flight of Soviet cosmonaut Yuri Gagarin in Nineteen Sixty One.

The first heart replacement surgery in the independent Kazakhstan was successful. The team, which performed the brilliant surgery did not disclose the results yet, continued to monitor the patient. It was obvious that results of their labor will be visible when Zhanibek will recover himself and begin to speak.

Is it easy to implant the heart taken from the dead body of the donor into the body of the recipient weakened by a prolonged illness?!

Zhanibek met the morning of the second day with his eyes open.

The exhausting illness as if had not happened. Heart is calm! Our prophet said, "In the human body there is a piece of flesh as big as a fist, if it's all right, the whole organism is healthy, this is the heart. A person with a pure heart will live a quiet life. And there is no greater happiness for the son of man than peace of mind." Has he reached this tranquility? Just thought about it, how the new heart beat joyfully. Before, the heart was beating very weakly, sometimes there was silence, as if it had stopped. In such moments, Zhanibek with feverish fingers felt the pulse on his neck and wrists. When he felt that it does not beat, he was frightened with cold sweat. Weakened even more. And now he realized that the heart was beating strongly and confidently, so much that it seemed as if it was ready to jump out of mouth.

It turns out that the heart gives birth to a craving for life!

He finally realized that he had survived an unprecedented surgery, was returned to a full life. He looked around the room. White walls. Warm rays of the August sun were pouring from the window. What a happiness it is to see the white light, feel involvement in this wonderful world.

Thank God! I Stayed alive! Oh, White Light, what a blessing to see you!

The jigit, inspired by joy, suddenly felt the smell of fried potatoes with meat. What a wonderful smell! He felt a strong desire to taste this dish. Potatoes and meat! How come, he likes dishes with broth! He considered fried food, a student food and did not particularly think of it. Knowing this, his wife tried to cook him good dishes with broth. There was no basis of an appetite for fried potatoes in the instant of coming-into-being.

Zhanibek did not understand that the craving for this food was born through a new heart inserted into him...

As can be seen from the world scientific news, after such surgeries patients get very different desires. Some want to drink water, the other – to smoke. And some feel the desire to drink beer. The practice of world transplantology shows that the recipient, as a rule, asks the donor's preferences.

After such heart transplantation, American citizen Debbie's life was filled with innovations. After the heart replacement surgery, the recipient who had never consumed alcohol expressed desire to drink beer. Besides, she, as turned out, did not like fried food sold on the streets, and after the surgery she felt an irresistible craving for it. She also changed musical preferences, she liked classics beforeand and began to listen to rap. Debbie associates all these changes with replacement of the heart and begins to learn the life of her donor.

Doctors in the United States do not suppress truth, they say whose heart saved her life. So, Debbie gets to know the family of 18-year-old black guy Howie, who crashed on a motorcycle, whose heart saved her life. It turned out that Howie adored street fried delicacies, beer and liked to listen to rap.

According to American professor Gary Schwartz, the heart is a powerful generator of electromagnetic energy. The magnetic force of the heart is 5000 times higher than the magnetic force of the brain. Therefore, according to the professor, this force is able to perform the role of a messenger of information to all corners of the body. Besides, Gary Schwartz believes that between the heart and the brain, in addition to the neural connection there are neurochemical and electrochemical connections. Therefore, the professor assumes that thoughts, feelings, fears, dreams and fantasies from the brain can go to the heart and remain there at the cellular level. And at heart transplant information can go into the brain of the recipient.

At that moment a group of people in white coats entered the door. They were the doctors and nurses who participated in the heart transplantation. From under the masks only the shine of eyes was seen. Kindness flows from their eyes, everyone looks at Zhanibek with love and joy.

Everybody is happy with the results of their unusual work.

As if expressing gratitude to the man for bravely enduring such torments;

No one said anything for a while, it was for the first time Zhanibek understood how it was possible to say so much silently with eyes. And his eyes shining from under thick eyebrows radiate on his saviors the rays of joy...

Zhanibek recognized each of them by their eyes.

At the head of the bed are Yuri Vladimirovich Pya and his Czech colleague Jan Pirk. Next are Bekbossynova Makhabbat Sansyzbaykyzy... Raikhan Rakhmatullakyzy... What kind radiant eyes... How good that his life was entrusted to these wonderful people...

It seems that he has just been in the operating room with them. Either in soul or body there is no trace of a six-hour battle for life and after a deep sleep for more than a day. Nothing hurts anywhere. The heart beats smoothly, the blood ripples even at the fingertips, from which they even itch. If they would have allowed he would immediately get out of bed and start doing something. A bright future is ahead...

Yuri Vladimirovich took Zhanibek's hands and asked in his gentle, sincere voice:

- "How are you, Zhanibek?"

- "Perfect! "– Zhanibek answered. His voice was a little indistinct and dull.

Endotriochial tube was still in his mouth. However, everyone realized that the answer was joyful and positive. Yuri Vladimirovich took the guy again by the hand and felt a slight shudder. So as to say, all is well.

The state of Zhanibek in those moments was really remarkable, which he tried to express in one word. This was his gratitude to his savior, coming from the depths of his soul. And the doctors were touched by the fact that he pronounced his first word after the surgery so emotionally with all his heart.

It was felt, the doctors were also satisfied that they managed, using knowledge and experience, thanks to patience and perseverance to save the patient's life and personally see the result of their work.

And the patient was content with being alive and being able now, with a new heart and new hopes, enter a new life he has never known before.

This feat, committed by the Yuri Pya team, raised the country's medicine to an unprecedented level. This was the clearest evidence that Kazakhstani transplant technologists know how to make such surgeries both technically and qualitatively.

President of the Republic of Kazakhstan, Nursultan Nazarbayev, having learned that such a unique surgery was carried out in our country, in our capital, the same day talked on the phone with the doctors saying that work of Yuri Vladimirovich Pya and his colleagues – people in white coats and with golden hands – raised the national medicine to the world level, that they are the pride of the Kazakh people. The Head of State voiced gratitude of the whole nation.

Yelbasy evaluated this medical achievement at a large republican forum saying, "The son of the Russian people passed the heart of his mother to a Kazakh, the kidneys to a German. The surgery was held by a Korean. This was an event demonstrating the unity of the Kazakh people."

"Indeed, medicine is rapidly developing today in Kazakhstan. But only recently aortocoronary shunting surgeries started. Today, several such operations are performed a day. He is confident that in the near future transplantation of an artificial heart will become a habitual matter.

Thank God, with the opening of a new cardiological center, things have improved significantly. It is possible to say with full certainty that the National Scientific and Cardiological Center in Astana meets all international standards. In the hospital, which was spread out on an area of 37 thousand square meters, 180 people can simultaneously get treatment, there are 6 operating units. All this makes it possible to annually hold up to 3000 open heart surgeries, carry out measures to ensure the normal operation of the heart vessels without opening the thoracic cavity. All equipment used is new – products of European companies "Siemens" and "Dreger."

Nursultan Abishevich on the day of familiarization with the construction of the building of this center said, "The main wealth for us is the health of the nation. We will not begrudge anything for this. Another big program is being implemented. Everything depends on you now." Head of the center Yuri Vladimirovich Pya, when he had an opportunity to speak, did not hide his joy. He said, with the opening of a specialized center, it will be possible to raise the cardiologic sphere to a new level, assured Yelbasy that the planned activities will certainly be carried out.

It will not be an exaggeration if we say that the center's eye-pleasing building became the dream of Kazakhstan cardiac surgeons. In this regard, the situation in the country used to leave much to be desired. Starting from the second half of the 20th century, cardiovascular diseases that swept the whole world were rapidly spreading in our country. According to medical reports, due to cardiovascular diseases up to 15 million people die each year in the world, and in Kazakhstan about 80 thousand people pass away for this very reason. All of them are people of working age of 35-60 years old. As a whole, in the republic, heart diseases are the first in terms of mortality. The scientists' forecasts for the future are not happy as well. According to them, a decline in cardiovascular diseases is not expected in the next thirty years. This can be understood from the fact that to date, 1 million 800 thousand residents of the republic are registered for cardiovascular diseases. How many people simply do not go to doctors? To improve the situation, it is necessary to do at least 15-16 thousand heart surgeries annually. And for this, of course, it is necessary to have a good material base, qualified doctors, funds – in a word, to develop the sphere of cardiac surgery. He repeatedly raised this problem at all meetings, relying on the experience of countries which he had occasion to visit. It turns out that this problem worried even Yelbasy. Therefore, the Head of State instructed the Government to elaborate a program for the development of the cardiosurgical sphere for 2007-2009 and take measures to implement it. The order was successfully executed. Today, cardiosurgical centers are being built not only in Astana, but also in regional centers. Now this sphere is so developed that all high technologies used in the world became available, they are in the inventory of the people of Kazakhstan.

The main goal of the center is to provide the population with qualified cardiological, cardiosurgical assistance, using innovative medical technologies. It has to be said, a lot has already been done in this regard. Each of the doctors of the center has sufficient experience, high professional training – they studied in leading clinics of the USA, Germany, Israel, Turkey, Lithuania, Russia and Belarus. They are Makhabbat Bekbossynova, Timur Lesbekov, Talgat Ibraev, Saltanat Zhetibayeva, Dmitry Gorbunov, Timur Kapyshev, Serik Bekbossynov, Yermagambet Kuatbayev, Muradym Oral-

bayev, Svetlana Novikova, Vladislav Achkassov, Yedil Botabayev, Darkhan Suygenbayev, Azamat Kurmalayev and Araigul Ydyryshova.

With the launch of the new center, thousands of patients were assisted, about four and a half thousand of them are adults, and one and a half thousand – children. Nearly 2000 patients underwent open heart surgeries, 500 of them to children and infants. In general, during this time, 50 types of additional blood circulation units were implanted in the center. This indicator should increase from year to year.

Indeed, today's situation cannot be compared with what was a year or two ago, a difference is like the earth and the sky. Besides, by using the ROC Safe system, the center has introduced a technology for performing cardiosurgeries. For those treated, this is a new, beneficial and safe technology. During surgeries with the use of this system, the need for artificial ventilation is reduced, the need for infusion of blood during the surgery and after it decreased. For the treatment of patients whose heart rhythms were violated, in the course of coronary artery bypass and heart valve replacement, they began to apply intra-operating radiofrequency ablation of Cardioblate system – innovative operating technology. In conjunction with endovascular surgeons, complex hybrid surgeries are performed on patients.

Another achievement of the center is that during the open-heart surgery, there was applied a method of extracorporeal membrane oxygen supply. In other words, patients with difficulty breathing during the surgery get oxygen injection by grafting into the blood. It should be noted that at the initiative of interventional surgery doctors, patients with congenital heart defect of a ventricle "bridge" started to be closed by trans-catheter – a new special technology.

Currently in Kazakhstan high-tech and multi-cardiac surgeries are made to children before one year old, infants with congenital heart disease and heart with a single ventricle. It is planned that patients with heart defects will get transplants, patients with defects of heart valves – prosthesis, minimally invasive endoscopic surgeries of the heart, high-quality assistance to children with arrhythmia, minimally invasive endovascular intervention. The center stated implementation of a scientific and technical project on the study of heart rhythm disturbances, genetic tendencies of its sudden stop. Implementation of this project will provide an opportunity to study the mechanism of development and causes of sudden cardiac arrest in people with atrial fibrillation and help to prepare new diagnostic methods," journalist Zharasbai Suleimenov wrote about today's achievements of domestic medicine in "Yegemen Kazakhstan" newspaper.

III

- "May I get up today and try to walk?" – Zhanibek asked a nurse, who was on duty in the morning of the third day after the surgery.

- "How to walk? Won't you weaken?"

- " My mother said that the more to lay, the more sickness is attached to a person. Maybe I'll try to stand up, leaning on you?" – he asked, almost begging.

- "For now, you can sit down and hang your legs from the bed. We will consult when the doctor comes. I don't know whether he will allow it or not, " - the nurse said, forbidding him to get up.

In the sitting position he felt more cheerful.

He looked outside the window. Light brown clouds floated across the sky. Nothing else was visible. Throwing back the sheet, he began to examine his body. The cut on the chest was tightly bandaged. No pain. The heart beats in a measured manner, even breathing. *Is it the heart beating very strongly or I'm just used to weak beats of a sick heart?* He thought, listening to his heart.

It was heartbeats of a person loving life! It gave him joy. Did the muscles of his hands, the wrists seemed puny? He crossed his arms, squeezed his muscles. Then his eyes fell to his legs – he was horrified. The flesh on the knees was flabby, the legs were thin, like the old man's. He touched his legs – only bones left! He touched his toes one by one. Skin and bones. Blue veins protrude above the fingers. Dr. Makhabbat Sansyzbaikyzy, who entered the room with a stethoscope on her neck, found him palping himself. Seeing him, sitting without a blanket she asked:

- "Zhanibek, what happened, is something bothering you?"
- "No, yes, my legs... too skinny, "- Zhanibek muttered.
- "Zhanibek, you underwent a very difficult surgery. Consider, anew born. Therefore, you lost a lot of weight. Now get up and look in the mirror, and then we'll weigh you up", she said in a cheerful tone, distracting him from examining his legs, helping him to stand up.

Zhanibek peered at the mirror the nurse gave him, saw a thin man with sunken eyes, sharpened cheekbones and hunchbacked nose. The nurse brought electronic scales, helped him to climb them. The scales showed 75 kilograms.

-" I lost eight kilograms in two or three days," - he said in a low voice.

- "Most importantly, your heart is new. Healthy! And you can overtake the weight with good food", Makhabbat Sansyzbaikyzy said, calming him down.

- "Oh, agay (older man), you found something to worry about, people can't lose weight! "– the nurse joked.

That day, Zhanibek, leaning on the nurse, took two steps with his thin legs and was completely exhausted...

Then, under the influence of sleeping pills, he spent the whole day half asleep. Taking medications, he lies for hours, trying to remember everything from his past life whence this illness was attached to him...

His mother Manuara Yeskalikyzy, was widowed at thirty-seven and was left with eight children. His father – Zeynel Seksenbayuly was director of a school in Yershovka village in the Uzynkol district of the Kostanay region, where many Russian people lived. He additionally taught history lessons. The father, being the only son among seven daughters, lived together with his elderly parents in a large, united family. Life was getting better; he became the best among his peers. However, a wound in the stomach suddenly inflamed and he passed away at less than forty.

Numerous relatives and households suddenly orphaned. Seven younger sisters and eight of his own children were left without reliable support. The youngest of the children was him – a two-year-old Zhanibek.

The things that his poor widowed mother endured early. After all, she was the daughter of the state farm director Yeskali Shaldybayev, who laid the basis of Taysoygan village in the Uzynkol district. She grew up without needing anything in a wealthy family. Then she married the most respected teacher of aul, the school headmaster. She became a re-spected mother, who gave birth to four sons and four daughters. Her husband's parents carried a single daughter-in-law almost in their hands, tenderly called her "Mantai." Apparently, it was fate that she was left alone early. She remained confused with eight children.

They had a grandmother in a large family , so the children, passing the kindergarten, immediately went to school. Two-year-old Zhanibek had to be sent to a kindergarten. Is it easy to feed such a horde of under-age children?! She rolled up her sleeves and went to work. But where can one go without special education, she had to start working at the grain receiving point of the village. And she worked there until she retired.

The children – one smaller than the other – did not sit idle: they raked snow, carried firewood, mowed hay – in a word, did everything that their father did while alive. As the saying goes, the poor get richer, orphans grow up. The children of Zeynel also grew up – each raised shanyrak, got their own family. Zhanibek grew up not lagging behind his peers. Although he did not aspire to get a higher education, he suc-cessfully graduated from the district center driving school, got a driver's license. He was called up for military service. He passed the medical commission without hindrances and went to serve. With the thought "So she brought her youngest up to adulthood," the joyful mother sent her son to the army. For the joy of the mother, Zhanibek was called to Derzhavinsk, which is next to Arkalyk – very near to home.

However, the mother's joy did not last long. A year later, Zhanibek, with swelling of both legs below the knees, was admitted to the medical unit. The medical commission found him unfit for military service and sent him home with a diagnosis of rheumatoid polyarthritis.

In his childhood he was fond of a motorcycle, he was outside for days in creaking Kostanai frosts. Often inflamed tonsils, often sick with sore throat. Maybe it influenced this.

The mother put him in the city hospital, bought a lot of medicines and somehow he was cured.

After that, until after thirty years old Zhanibek forgot about his illness. He worked as a driver at the plant. Got married in Arkalyk, became a father – his wife gave birth to a girl. To be honest, life did not improve, and they had to divorce. All these troubles made not only the mother to suffer, but also beat his own heart.

Exhausted by the disease he decided to turn to the Republican National Medical Center. Doctors of the center examined him, diagnosed, prescribed various medications and dismissed him. He took medicine for a while, and then stopped. The heart no longer seemed to bother him, and he calmed down on it.

A divorced, lonely guy moves to the city of Rudny. Maybe bachelor life affected him, but soon his health reminded of itself. The local cardiologist once again warned that his heart has serious defects.

Let's face it, we do not always pay attention to the work of our heart with the size of a fist. It ensures blood circulation in the body all life, does not stop for a second. Only sometimes, with excitement or joy, we feel that it is ready to jump out of the chest. This is a familiar phenomenon.

And when, irrespective of the state of the soul, the rhythm of its beating is broken: it starts to beat either too often, or slowly, and sometimes it stops, then each of us should think. In such cases, immediate doctor consultation is needed.

Zhanibek's heart beats began to weaken, interruptions appeared.

An incomprehensible cough appeared. One day at the end of the working day the cough increased, his head reeled and he fell. People around him frightened by blood from his mouth called an ambulance and he got taken to the intensive care unit.

Thank God, with the help of doctors at that time, Zhanibek Ospanov stayed alive. After he came to himself, he was sent to the Republican National Medical Center. After a long examination in the center, they decided to install a *pacemaker* on the heart. What is it – was explained to the patient .

A pacemaker is a small electrical appliance that stimulates the heart. It is sewn into the chest or under the skin around the abdomen. The pacemaker is connected to the heart by one or two wires (electrodes), often through the blood vessels. The function of the stimulator is to prevent the heart beat from falling below a certain level. Equipped with special detectors, it tracks the work of the heart, the speed of strokes. If the beats slow down, the stimulator turns on and sends small electrical impulses to the heart. These impulses through the electrodes reach the heart and encourage it to work in the right rhythm. And if on the contrary, ripple becomes excessively high, then the stimulator automatically turns off. In other words, it works only in necessary cases.

Implantation of a stimulant is an easier surgery than the heart surgery. The implantation was carried out in a special ward of the Cardiac Center equipped with X-ray equipment. The surgery was conducted under local anesthesia, Zhanibek felt cheerful. Perhaps the most difficult thing was to lie on his back without moving for a long time. He withstood it, consider, successfully withstood the surgery!

It turns out that with such stimulants people live for decades. People get so used to the pacemaker that they forget that it is wired into the body. As usual they go to work, use public transport. Go swimming, bathe in the bathroom. Even perform marital duties. There are many cases when young women with stimulants got pregnant, safely giving birth to healthy children.

The doctors explained to Zhanibek in detail how to perform antibiotic therapy without fail. With a wired pacemaker, the man went home. He spent two years with this device. He had to quit driver's work, as he became an invalid of the second group.

In appearance, Zhanibek Ospanov had no shortcomings. By burning eyes, thick eyebrows one can judge that the man has a real masculine temper.

Cheerful mood, propensity for jokes, desire for life returned with the installation of the device, restoration of health. At this time in the seventy-first year of her life mother Manuara died, who for all her life with all her heart worried about her darling youngest son. This somewhat shattered him, he felt completely alone. The apartment, which for him and his mother seemed a khan's palace, suddenly became empty.

During these woeful days he met a young teacher Munira, who was seven years younger than him, a very warm relationship was established. He did not hide anything from the girl, told about his health. He also told about the pacemaker in the chest. Munira was sensible, she listened calmly. Firmly, without hesitation said:

- "I love you the way you are!"

- "Munira, you know that today medicine is developing well , it is time for new technologies. All these achievements are being adopted in Kazakhstan. Don't think that I will wear this device all my life. I think that doctors will find the means to cure me of this ailment. Whatever the treatment is, I will go for it, I will agree! "– Zhanibek firmly mannishly promised.

Munira is a Kazakh language and literature teacher. She read everything from the verses and words of Abay to the modern Kazakh literature, she can tell and unscramble everything.

Zhanibek graduated from the Russian school. He likes to read classical works. He knows world literature. When Munira starts watching the series, Zhanibek offers to watch the Soviet epic film on the novel by Anatoly Ivanov "Eternal Call." He never tired of watching a film about the fate of the Saveliev brothers Anton, Fedor and Ivan. Through the eyes of brothers who lived through three wars, he went into history, loved to learn about today's life. It talked his native language, but so to say, didn't know literature. Munira filled this gap.

Once she read:

The sick heart beats softly

In the tired chest, not raging,

Blood hot pours it,
In the sleepless nights, not knowing rest.

(interlinear translation)

First, Zhanibek didn't understand, but when rereading, he liked poetry.

- "Read it again! "– He asked. When reading for the third time he was impressed.

- "Whose?" – he asked.

- "Do you know Abay?" – the girl asked.

- "Of course, why should I not know,"" – the jigit was offended.

From this day on, they began to talk about Kazakh literature, look for certain books, read them. During the Soviet Union, books were published in thousands of copies, reaching the most remote auls. Today, books are published at best in the amount of three thousand copies, all of them are mostly left to the customers themselves. And today the right books are scarcely in sight. Young people find what they need on the Internet. Zhanibek also adapted to search in the Internet, typing in the word *heart* in search. He didn't want to lag behind Munira. One day friends gifted him a book where he saw the poem "Zhuregime" ("To my heart"), he read it several times. It struck him. It was as if about his heart:

> Gurgling in mother's womb,
> My heart, you were born before me.
> You knew what love is before me,
> You were called life before me.
>
> When you're beating on my left,
> I aspire to peaks and races.
> From you originates, my heart,
> In my chest is a raging verse.

Sometimes you overshadow my mind,
You make me incapable of anything.
Sometimes you roll to my throat,
Feeling good and evil before me.

Thanks to you I have known love,
I despised and hated though you.
I laid my head at stake,
Torturing you, I avenged my grievances.

You have endured so many trials,
You look for answers to a lot of questions.
You disperse my blood through the veins,
You are the beginning of a spring called life.

(interlinear translation)

- Indeed, when a new life appears in the womb, the heart signals the first signs of life with a heartbeat. Life begins from it. Today, ultrasound examination, rhythmic beats of the future baby's heart can be heard. And the small body of a child, movements can be felt only after three months, - this is what Zhanibek thought, before Munira called. Zhanibek jumps up and hurries to meet his beloved to share his impressions of what he read during the day...

That year they got married. His sick heart was joined by the loving heart of Munira, his head was spinning with happiness, he completely forgot about the device that was in his chest.

IV

Two years after the pacemaker was installed in the chest, in one of the May days , the heart felt hot and a shiver appeared. Habitually he got his things and went to Astana by train. He came to the Republican

National Medical Center for examination. That time, the arrhythmic doctor informed that a new Cardiology Center was open and additional consultations could be held there.

In the new center, Cardiologist Saltanat Yerkhankyzy received him and after a long examination said that the device is working properly, but the heart itself gets weaker every year. She explained that if this continues, the heart will not last long. A diagnosis "chronic terminal heart failure" was made. 80-90 percent of people affected by this disease die not living a year. Nothing the doctor hid, she concluded: the only way is to replace the heart. Then she told him to come in early August to the center for treatment.

At home together with Munira, they began to search for all heart-related news. It turns out, many of these innovations are already being applied in our country, but replacement of the heart – transplantology has not yet been reached. And if Zhanibek's heart will not get better after treatment, it will have to be changed. For this it is necessary to go abroad. And where to get money for this. These days up to thirty thousand tenge go towards medications monthly. He himself is an invalid of the second group. The only breadwinner at home is Munira, who works as a teacher and must go on maternity leave soon.

- "Let's look for a sponsor for going abroad," - the young woman suggests.

- :"There are many people like me, everyone is looking for sponsors. Is it possible to help everyone? Open any newspaper, any TV channel, everywhere disabled people and seriously ill patients are looking for sponsors," - the husband answered despondently in a hopeless voice.

In such arguments time passed, August came. In the family, usually before the long journey or beginning of any big business, they went to the graves of the father and mother, read prayers and gave memorial dinners. Observing the custom, together with his wife they went to Yershovka, read prayers, got the blessing of the elders.

On the day of returning home in the morning, Munira saw a dream.

... Zhanibek allegedly having returned from a long journey. Undressed to the waist was engaged in housework. Munira looked at his chest. Earlier on the left side of the chest there was a trace from the pacemaker in the form of a dash. There were no dashes. The body was smooth, and he looked strong.

- "Munira, I'll never be sick! A miracle happened! "- he says, playing as an athlete with his elastic muscles.

Probably, the spirits of ancestors will support and he will recover, - she thought and woke up.

Inspired by hope, overcome by doubts, Zhanibek left for Astana to treat his sick heart.

About the pregnant women, Kazakhs usually say, "one foot is on the ground, the other is in the grave," despite the fact that there were only a few days left until the birth, Munira remained alone in Rudny. She asked her husband not to worry about her and wished him to be well cured.

From the first days of being in the Republican National Scientific and Cardiological Center, Zhanibek felt that this time his health survey was done a little differently. Every day he takes several tests. Medicines gave more results. He slept peacefully, and often saw dreams. The excitement did not pass. There seems to be nothing to worry about his wife – they talked on the phone several times a day. Talked with her every day, as if he did not leave home.

He told her that in a dream he sailed on the sea and was often panting. Munira, as an old lady, explained his dream this way, "You are suffocating because your heart beats at night, the sea and water are signs of longevity."

Early in the morning of the third day, nurses warned him: don't eat, they will make heart coronarography.

They took him to a special room, the doctor made a local anesthetic, attached glue tubes to his legs. They gave anesthetic injection. Contrast fluid was poured into the artery of the heart through the catheter. Then they took a picture of the heart. The condition of blood vessels was examined.

In the morning, several cardiologists came and asked about everything. Nurses one by one came in, took blood from hands, from fingers.

Doctors, headed by Yuri Vladimirovich Pya, chairman of the board of "National Scientific and Cardiological Center" JSC, held special consultation on health status of Zhanibek Ospanov. Consulting physician Raikhan Rakhmatullakyzy, proceeding from the consultation conclusions asked Zhanibek, "Would you agree to a transplantation – your sick heart replacement to a healthy one?"

- "Is my heart so hopeless?" – the man asked.

- "It turns out so. It is not good for shunting. It can hardly withstand six months."

- "For such a surgery it is necessary to go abroad, I have no such possibility," the man said sadly.

- "And if we conduct this surgery in our center, would you agree?"

- "For this, first of all, you need to have a heart! "– he exclaimed, remembering how many patients are standing in line for the donor body.

- "We have a heart, so there is an opportunity to transplant it to you. This will be the first heart replacement surgery in our country. If you trust, Yuri Vladimirovich with his team is ready to proceed. We invited a colleague from the Czech Republic who has experience in such surgeries."

- "How much time do I have to think about it? "– asked Zhanibek as any man who loves particularity in business.

- "Time's running out. You must make decision within two hours. This morning, a 46-year-old woman died from brain hemorrhage. Her heart is in good condition. Her kidney will be transplanted to a person who is suffering like you are. The son of this woman extended humanity and agreed to give his mother's heart. Therefore, in the morning we took all the tests from you, checked the immunological compatibility. All indicators coincide. The structure of her body tissue also coincides with yours. You can say, lucky you. If you agree we proceed immediately. We can't stall – the heart can die... With whom should you consult?"

- "My wife is nine months pregnant. In Kostanai my elder sister and son-in-law live, I will consult with them. "

Such a short conversation took place between the patient and the doctors. First Zhanibek spoke with his son-in-law Bolat on mobile phone. Explained the situation. Bolat, whose wife was sick for many years and understood what it is, said, "If your own heart is hopeless, agree. Decide youself. The best counselor for a person is himself."

Then he called to Munira. "If you are standing, sit down, make yourself comfortable and listen," he told his wife. Munira was always a calm person. Another would, perhaps, reproach, "What good I saw, marrying you, all the money goes to your medication. I also need to eat well, I need to dress beautifully, I need... I need..." Human needs, especially women are endless. And she is happy that Zhanibek, at least alive, satisfied with the small things that God sent.

Zhanibek fully conveyed his dialogue with the doctors. He said that he had spoken with his son-in-law Bolat, then he asked, "What do you say? There is not enough time for reflection, let's make decision sooner!"

What can a pregnant woman advise immediately. "In any case, I need you alive. I pray to God about this," she answered and began to cry.

He listened to the advice of the closest people – the son-in-law Bolat and his beloved wife, they say – decide for yourself. For the Kazakh, *decide for yourself* are hard words. This means that in any situation, the responsibility lies with yourself. Whatever happens – only yourself is responsible.

Time was approaching. Zhanibek walked for a while back and forth in the ward. Then, remembering that he had not asked everything, he ran into the staff room. He found Raikhan Rakhmatullakyzy and showered her with questions.

- "Who is a woman by nationality, whose heart you intend to insert?"

- "Russian."

- "So, of another faith, doesn't this contradict Islam?"

- "Zhanibek, I cannot answer such a question. I'm a doctor. I look at you and her like at patients. There is no concept of a border, another faith, another nationality and even an enemy for a doctor. Doctors have only one goal – to save lives, for this the doctor goes for everything, "- the doctor explained.

- "What did she die of?"

- "Stroke. Hemorrhage in the brain."

- "Hemorrhage not from vodka?"

- "No. She was a teacher, an intelligent person. Blood pressure rose because of the heat, she fell unconscious and didn't leave the coma."

- "I'm a man, she's a woman, won't it affect my nature later?"

- "You take from her only the organ – the heart. And the heart is a kind of motor that drives blood through the body. You do not change sex," - laughed the doctor, understanding his hidden thoughts.

Zhanibek smiled too.

- "If you want, I'll invite a psychologist, "- the doctor said.

- "Not necessary. I believe you. I agree! "– he said holding out his hand, weakened from the disease. The doctor slightly squeezed his hand by her two hands and said:

- "Don't be nervous and don't worry. If you are confident in yourself, everything will be fine!"

He remembered the fairy tales that the mother told him: "With the cry "Nartauekel!" batyrs entered the battle."

"Bismillah!" – said the grandmother before starting any work.

Nartauekel! (which roughly means "Whatever will happen!" "Risk is a noble cause," – translator).

Bismillah!

With a confident hand, he signed all the conciliatory documents brought by Makhabbat Sansyzbaikyzy.

In the morning, along with two doctor-professors from the Czech Republic, Yuri Vladimirovich entered the room. The doctors looked confident, determined. This confidence seemed to be passed to Zhanibek, inspired him. After talking a little more about the forthcoming surgery, the doctors left.

Zhanibek was visited by his older sister and son-in-law Bolat. In a cheerful tone, wishing to raise the mood of Zhanibek, they told various funny stories and left, wishing him the support of Allah and the spirits of their ancestors.

He talked on the phone with his wife, told her a lot of kind words. Munira, like an intelligent woman, did not say a word about the surgery, she talked about the future child. If she were a weak woman, she would burst into tears. And he would have got discouraged.

If I only stay alive after this surgery, Zhanibek thought, I will do everything possible to ensure that Munira and the child are happy. And I'll take care of the girl that is left with her mother.

His mental communication with relatives was interrupted by nurses. They made an injection and smeared the chest with iodine. In a while he was drawn to sleep.

Then an anisiologist came along with the nurse. The arrival of the anthysiologist meant one thing – the time of the surgery is near.

Zhanibek took a deep breath, said "Bismillah!" and sat in a wheelchair.

Soon the trolley on which he was lying was rolled toward the operating unit...

V

The heat did not drop - it was hell all over Sary-Arka today too.

People probably inhale not the air, but fire, Galina Konstantinovna thought, walking out onto the street. In the yard she tapped water into a jug and began to pour a thin stream on the head. She seemed to feel better, sat down on a bench in the courtyard under a sprawling oak tree. Flies and mosquitoes too were tired out, sitting on her face and on her neck.

She felt giddy.

Her heart began to beat fast, she began to suffocate. In the morning she felt trouble. Worried for Igor, who went to Astana, thanks to the daughter she called the phone. "Everything is fine with me. How are you there, does anything worry you, has pressure gone down? Today, they say, the heat will reach forty degrees. After lunch, as I finish my work, I'll go home," the son said. After that she calmed down, sitting, remembering different things.

I don't feel well. All summer pressure goes up and down. Treatment in the hospital didn't help. What will happen to you, if anything happens to me. And you don't have a father. From the only mother you have only this small house. And there are no regular documents to formalize your inheritance, the woman thought. She got up, was going home, but felt giddy.

- "Daughter, Vera! Vera!" – cried the woman and fell backwards in the yard. Slippers from her feet and the jug flew apart. A small blond girl heard a desperate cry and the sound of fall of the obese body – she ran outside.

- "Mama! Mama!" cried the girl. Raised her mother's head and asked, looking into her eyes:

- "Mom, what's wrong? Say something!"

At the cry of the girl, an old woman-neighbour ran in.

- "Galya ... Galya," - she whispered, lifting her head.

Veronica ran home and called her brother on the mobile phone.

Igor reached the farthest state farm of the Tselinograd district of the Akmola region earlier than the ambulance. The mother was taken to the district hospital in his friend's car.

Doctors have identified a specific diagnosis: a stroke. She was urgently taken to Astana in an ambulance.

He was already an adult guy and understood everything that had happened, and he did not have the confidence that his mother would be able to get out of the coma, this made his heart break with despair.

- "Poor mother! – What did she see in this life. Always tried to feed us, put us on our feet and brought herself to such a state! "- he shared with his friend.

- "Don't worry, everything will be fine," - the friend consoled.

- "No, my heart feels trouble," - Igor burst into tears.

- "In any case, my mom tried to be the best. As a child she was a talented girl, she drew very well. After graduation she entered the Vasily Ivanovich Surikov Moscow Art Institute. But after the second year she had to quit school because of the illness of our grandmother. Later she graduated from the Almaty Pedagogical Institute. However, she dreamed of becoming an artist all her life. With tears in her eyes she remembered the days of her studies in Moscow. In school, dreaming to instill sense of beauty in children, she additionally taught drawing lessons. She wanted me and Vera to get good education. When I finished school, there was a so-called testing and I did not pass for the grant study. Mom, saying that *I should study, nothing will begrudge for me*, she arranged for me paid study in the Kazakh-Russian University. I can imagine how hard the poor mother got this money!" - the son cried all the way.

In the Republican Scientific Center of Neurosurgery Galina Vorotnikova with a diagnosis of stroke was immediately put into surgery. Stroke (Latin insulto – attack, leap) is a very dangerous disease lasting more than 24 hours or leading to instantaneous death, characterized by sudden loss or impairment of brain functions, leading to pathology of brain vessels. There are two types of stroke: hemorrhagic (burst blood vessels and hemorrhage) and ischemic (blockage of blood vessels). Doctors explained to Igor that in most cases, hemorrhagic stroke occurs due to high blood pressure.

Vorotnikova fell into coma because of hemorrhagic type of stroke.

Coma *(coma – deep sleep) – complete loss of consciousness, lack of response to external stimuli, dysfunction of the central nervous system.*

Neurosurgeons fully and in detail explained to Igor the state of his mother and reported that with all the diligence of the doctors her brain died. It was time to disconnect her from the life support apparatus.

In medicine, there is the notion of a "potential donor." "Potential donor" is only a patient in a state of "dead brain." When heart works, lungs get forced ventilation, and brain completely stops functioning, it means death of a person.

As experts say, according to clinical signs, special commission of doctors makes a conclusion about brain death by conducting electroencephalography and angiography.

To avoid the question "How does it turn out that the human brain dies before the person?" let us turn to science.

This concept was introduced in 1959 by French neuropathologists. In 1966, Pope Pius XII defined death as the separation of the soul from the body. Therefore, the diagnosis of "brain death" has no relation with transplantation, is considered an independent diagnostic procedure. After making such a diagnosis, all resuscitation measures stop. And heart, liver and other organs, blood circulation of the person who should become a donor continue to function, supported by special devices. However, they work for a certain period. During this period, these organs must be transplanted to another person. Experts believe that a "potential donor" can prolong life to at least four patients. Today it is well known that a person over 60 cannot be a donor. Organs also get old! Besides, it turns out, there are people whose internal organs wear out in forty years or so.

In other words, not just anyone can be a donor.

The fact that Galina Vorotnikova was suitable for donation was great happiness for Zhanibek and Yevgeny – they were destined to live in this world.

The next day, a freelance transplant from the Ministry of Health Gani Kuttymuratov arrived and spoke with the closest relative of the deceased – Igor, Vorotnikova's son. He explained to her son that although his mother's brain died, her heart and kidneys continue to work, are in good condition and, if he agrees, can continue to live in the body of another person. *By the will of fate he lost his mother, but it will be a manifestation of great humanity to save the lives of fathers of other families.*

Igor's heart was bursting with grief, with pity for his mother, with the tears of his inconsolable sister. He was pondering walking along the corridor a while.

The heart was asked for a Kazakh man, in this connection he remembered mother's stories...

Only in the spring in the circle of relatives, son and daughter, poor mother celebrated her forty-fifth anniversary!

She was greatly respected by numerous students and their parents. As if feeling that this was her last birthday, everyone tried to show what he was capable of. What a happy day Galina Konstantinovna had! How happy was mother, who hadn't seen such happy moments in her life, such a holiday! *The only joy of life was her little daughter and fast growing-up son – her future support in her old age.*

Galina Konstantinovna was a very good-natured, simple-hearted woman. She was generous, she didn't begrudge anything from anyone, she shared her last. Igor's father ascended to the Russian nobility. Grandmother during the Stalinist repressions was exiled to ALZHIR from Leningrad with two children.

ALZHIR – "Akmola camp for wives of traitors of the Motherland" by the NKVD order was established in 1938 and operated until 1953. About 20,000 wives and relatives of Stalinist repressions were held in it, under inhuman conditions. ALZHIR was called "hell on earth."

His grandmother, after she was rehabilitated, remained to live in the village Malinovka. She stayed with two children among the Kazakhs and found a common language with them. Moreover, a local Kazakh man, Taygar liked the beautiful Russian woman. They started a family.

My grandmother gave birth to two more sons from the Kazakh. The Vorotnikovs communicate with the children of Taigar until now. Daughter Zhanna, as the elder sister of Igor often visited them. Because of this story the mother had a special attitude to Kazakhs. Mother often said to Igor: *learn the Kazakh language, grandmother knew it well. The history of Kazakhstan is the history of your Motherland.* Fulfilling the mother's order, Igor tried to learn the Kazakh language, he understood it freely. And history was his favorite subject from his school days.

Thinking about all this, he tried to look at the offer of the transplantologist from his mother's perspective.

After all, the mother, if was possible, helped everyone!

She brought up her children like that. If the brain is dead, let healthy heart and kidney live, rather than they will rot under the earth! He took decision: *if there is an opportunity, why not make someone happy. No matter how sorry for his mother he was, nothing can be changed.* After consulting with his sister Veronika, he made the final decision: let the beating HEART and health KIDNEY continue to live on.

By Igor's decision, mother Galina Konstantinovna Vorotnikova, gave a heart to Zhanibek Ospanov, and the kidney – to Yevgeny Kurtz, she went to another world, giving them life…

As soon as the donor's relative gave his consent, doctors immediately began to conduct angiographic examination of Galina Vorotnikova, they found that there were no bruises in the arteries of the brain, the heart was clean. Not seeing any danger, they immediately began to withdraw the organ.

VI

Zhanibek was in a separate room under the watchful eye of specialists. A nurse was nearby. At the slightest deviation from the norm, they urgently started examination.

On the third day he quietly began to get out of bed and slowly, uncertainly stepping his feet, move around the ward.

He was reminded of a just born camel. Panting appeared. Knees were shaking.

The heart was beating smoothly. The pulse was rhythmic.

The discolored fingers and toes began to come to life, tingling and itching a little from the blood.

The nails were blue, now they gradually began to blush.

The blue lips were often cracked, they were now wet and almost crimson.

With the escaping of anesthesia from the body, sleep began to disappear, muscles and sometimes bones ached. Chronic rheumatism also reminded him of itself, the joints swelled. The doctors intensified treatment. Every half hour they made injections and put infusions.

Zhanibek stayed in intensive care for two weeks. To somehow distract the attention of the patient, on the instructions of Yuri Vladimirovich a big wall-TV was mounted. Until bedtime the patient spent days moving through television channels.

One day, during his uncertain walk, Makhabbat Sansyzbaikyzy looked into the room. Joyfully, as the mother looks at the first steps of her son, she watched the movements of Zhanibek. Her eyes radiated joyfully over the mask-bandage. She looked like a gardener who was enjoying the fruits of labor...

- "How are you, Zhanibek? " – she asked in a soft, sympathetic maternal voice.

- "Good."

- "They say you didn't sleep last night."

- "I didn't want to sleep."

- "Is something bothering you?" – asked the discerning doctor, as if reading" Zhanibek's thoughts.

- "I'm worried about my wife," - Zhanibek confessed. – "She is at the ninth month, if contractions start in Rudny, who will take care of her?... All relatives are all in Kostanai..."

- "I see you started to recover. You are not worried about yourself yet, but you worry like a husband and father. Don't worry, I'll make sure that Munira is brought here. Until he gives birth, she will be with you in Astana, "- she said.

Makhabbat Sansyzbaikyzy kept her word – Munira was taken to Astana. They placed her in a separate ward. He was immensely pleased with this. To be honest, he was afraid: *they say people love with their heart, but what if someone else's heart will not recognize Munira, will he treat his relatives coldly?* And his heart, as wanting to calm him down, at the sight of his wife aroused itself, as if it rushed to meet her. At that time he lay in bed, his heart beat joyously, as if wanted to jump out of his mouth.

Munira burst into tears of joy, tears poured on her medical mask. Makhabbat Sansyzbaikyzy warned both not to worry much. Keeping this in mind, both tried to restrain themselves.

What happiness it is to feel alive again, lie holding hand of a loved one!

He just thought that as the lump rose in his throat and Zhanibek sobbed involuntarily. He could not restrain himself.

- "Come on, Zhanibek, don't cry, I'm here. The most important you are alive. Soon our baby will be born. Will grow her together, "- Munira consoled him.

Zhanibek still could not come to his senses, stop, his chin shuddered in a silent sob.

Makhabbat Sansyzbaikyzy came running. She immediately began to count the pulse, listened to his heart. And Zhanibek was still crying.

-"What's wrong you, Zhanibek? Your wife came. You are alive and well. Is there something hurting you?" – the cardiologist was completely worried.

- "No, nothing. What about the children of the woman who gave me her heart? "– he asked, and again starter crying.

Zhanibek was depressed.

His hands were trembling, his chin was trembling, crooked.

He wanted to cry for no reason.

He couldn't understand his condition. Doctors were afraid that his condition will affect the heart; they called a special doctor for diseases of the nervous system.

Today in the world depression is in the second place after heart disease. In other words, society is worried about depletion of the nervous system of mankind. According to world statistics, 25 percent of suicide is due to depression.

It turns out that all mental illnesses are divided into neurosis and psychosis. Neurosis (depression, stress, dysthymia, etc.) can be detected in almost any person. It is known that dependence on money, dependence on time, insecurity immerse a person in imaginary fear and panic. Parting with a loved one, bad boss, divorce, hard work, lack of money give rise to fright and lead to illness. Psychosis for the most part can be hereditary or a consequence of an accident, head injury or infection.

The doctor-psychotherapist, who examined Zhanibek, defined his depression as neurosis. It depends not only on the current state of the guy, but also may be due to the fate of the heart that Galina Vorotnikova gave him . It remained young a single mother wishing to provide children with comfort life; she may have depleted the nervous system.

When he thought, "What happiness it is to feel alive again, lie holding hand of a loved one!" perhaps, in the depths of heart there was bitterness of a woman, whose beloved was ill, could not be there, leaving her life not putting two children on their feet, other unfulfilled desires and dreams. Probably, these unfulfilled dreams and unattained goals of two people – the donor and the person who took someone else's heart – hurt his heart, makes him cry, causes shiver in his hands.

In this regard, American professor Gary Schwartz argues that in addition to the neural connection between the heart and the brain, there are also neurochemical and electrochemical bonds. Therefore, thoughts, feelings, fears, dreams and fantasies of a person from the brain can be transmitted to the cells of the heart, stored there, and then after heart transplant are transmitted to the brain of that person, the professor assumes.

For the first time among the CIS countries, heart surgery was performed in Ukraine at the A.Shalimov Institute of National Surgery and Transplantology. Ukrainian psychotherapist Marina Yushko says: heart replacement surgery is a very complicated surgery. The human brain is like a computer, it is not yet known how it will perceive disconnection and re-activation. This person, in fact, died and came to life again. Having taking out his sick heart, they put a healthy one, but someone else's heart. This process is very complex and has not been fully investigated to the end. Therefore, a person who changed his heart, can have new properties of nature, arise new interests. The reason is simple: all mechanisms get ignition from the new "motor"…

Each organism is special in its own way. There are no identical hands and feet, pupils of eyes and other organs. All of us are born with a psychomatrix peculiar only to us. Imagine a hologram. If you destroy this picture, then any part of it will show the same picture. The heart resembles one of the parts of that hologram. Therefore, M.Yushko writes, in such situation the recipient can feel some life circumstances of the donor.

A variety of thoughts about the heart come over Zhanibek, "Someone else's heart is in my chest. The heart of another person. If a person becomes a mother or a father to a stranger, he/she is called a stranger – stepmother or stepfather. And the child will be a stranger for them: stepdaughter or stepson.

Stranger mother … stranger father… stranger child…

In the relationships of these three creatures, there are feelings of alienation, allogeneity and a kind of strangeness. Of course, not all are the same. There are women close as a mother, there are men who become closer them own father, and children – dear as their own. And will my heart, since it is not native, show its alienity?! "No, I'd rather wish it to become my native. It should not be alien to me…," he thought at moments of insomnia. He laid his hands on his chest, as if embracing his heart and as if saying: relate with my body, mate with my soul and blood, and then he lay listening to his heartbeat.

Sometimes, as if something bothered him, he would wake up in the middle of the night. Then he asked his heart, "What happened? What's bothering you? We should not let down those who believe in us. Don't be ill, don't shy away from my body, get used to it faster. I'll love you. You're the most important organ in my body. You beat – I live. Be merciful," he told his heart.

He started to see a lot of dreams. Just closed his eyes, as if watching a movie...

He happens in places where he's never been in his life, communicates with people of European appearance. Dreams are colorful, vivid. He tries to peer into them through eyes of an artist, remember each landscape, remember them. He admires the big city where he has never been. These are probably the deep memories of Galina Vorotnikova, her secret dreams that have not come true...

Twice or thrice a week a psychologist comes, talks with him on various instructive topics, answers Zhanibek's questions, makes him take various tests.

He lost a lot of weight: his legs became like matches, his shoulders bulge with bones. For his happiness, the surgery wound healed quickly. His deceased mother said, "Until you reached forty days of your life I bathed you in salt water. And that's why any of your cuts and burns heal quickly." Probably, she was right – the seam on his chest began to itch and heal.

Bedsores formed from a constant long-term lying on his back. Deposition of salts on shoulders and neck worried him, old disease of osteochondrosis bothered him, and weak flow of blood into the head tormented him. Makhabbat Sansybaikzyzy found ways to solve these problems as well. Every three hours they massaged his back dispersing stagnant blood and salt...

From long periods sitting next to Zhanibek, worrying for him, Munira had, so-called, false labor. Previously, our mothers called this phenomenon *aitolgaq*.

Munira told Makhabbat Sansyzbaikyzy about her condition, who immediately contacted Tamara Anatolyevna Vaschenko from the National Mother and Child Center and called for an ambulance.

After staying in the center for about two weeks, on August 27, Munira safely gave birth to a healthy girl.

Makhabbat Sansyzbaikyzy came to Zhanibek to ask for "suyunshi" – to tell the glad tidings. The new heart started up as a joyful bird as if informing it belonged under it. Noticing this, the doctor shook his hand, congratulated and said:

- "Zhanibek, don't worry much, everything's all right. Progeny continues. Your health is the bright future of your daughter."

Twenty days later, Zhanibek already went outside, stepping his feet on the ground, inhaling fresh air and bathing in the sun.

He thanked every living day, waking up in the morning he went to the window and looked outside for a long time. He looked carefully at the people coming in and out of the center doors. In the course of this illness, he fully understood what a great happiness it is to be healthy, to walk on the ground. He felt he was born again, he was glad that with the heart of another person he woke up healthy every morning. He seemed just to understand the mother's blessing, "Let the people be prosperous, and you be healthy in it!" What can be better, when your homeland is united, your people are calm and you live safely in this country too! He begins to understand words of his mother that "any troubles you experience together with the people are like a holiday." It turns out that the wisdom is true that any hardships or difficulties must be experienced together with the people. Unlike others, his heart ached, tormented by his soul, he's almost been beyond the veil. Everyone but him seemed happy. He seemed to be the only unhappy one, bound to bed. Looking out the window, he then dreamed of plunging in the crowd of happy and carefree people and experience with them all the joys of life. It turned out this day was not far off. If twenty days ago he went to bed with *fear for tomorrow*, now he met every morning with the thought what *today has prepared for me.* Every sunny morning seems to pour force into the body, leading to a new bright life...

- "Your first direction after the surgery will go to the National Mother and Child Center, where you will see the continuation of your life," Makhabbat Sansyzbaikyzy unexpectedly cheered him up.

One of the nurses equipped Zhanibek as an astronaut: put on mask in his face, pulled on clothes that looked like a whole-jumpsuit. Attending physician Saltanat Kozhikovna, cardiac surgeon Serik Temirkhanuly, who brought him a donor heart, and Makhabbat Sansyzbaikyzy – the three of them went to the center where Munira gave birth.

When they were already approaching the center, Serik Temirkhanuly handed Zhanibek an armful of flowers, which he held in his hands.

- "Hand it to your wife," he said, and jokingly asked: "Did you give her flowers before?"

- "When I worked at the dacha, returning home, I tore free flowers and brought them to her. I didn't buy flowers intentionally," - the guy confessed.

- "Aul jigits cannot deceive with flowers, as you, "- struck back colleague Makhabbat Sansybaikyzy. – "They bring their hearts."

Colleagues from the National Mother and Child Center headed by Tamara Anatolyevna with open arms met guests from the National Scientific and Cardiological Center on the porch.

When cardiac surgeons performed a feat in their field, raising the glory of republican medicine to an unprecedented height, they did not stay aloof – they helped to give birth to the wife of the first person whose heart was replaced safely. Such a historical circumstance cannot be purposefully organized. This was an amazing event, which fell only on the share of Zhanibek. It so happened that he was born with his child, this probably happens only with one in a hundred million people. Thanks to introduction of this miracle into history, noble people in white coats from the National Scientific and Cardiological Center and the National Mother and Child Center lit the rays of hope in souls and revived a high dream.

Blonde by nature, thin Munira became white and even more skinny. Is it easy for a young woman, without sleeping, on the one hand, to think about health of her husband and on the other – to worry about successful childbirth? Young women – even whose husbands are quite healthy – suffer until the end of labor. And how many sleepless nights she spent alone at home in Rudnoye, when her husband was between life and death, when she asked for help from one Allah only! How many tears she shed in the pillow ...

All this is now behind: she gave birth safely, presses the baby to her breast and meets her beloved husband. Zhanibek, whose eyes glittered joyfully from under the mask, was dressed all in white among doctors in white coats. And when he took the child carefully from his wife hands, his heart agitated, tears involuntarily came in his eyes. He looked at the child with tear-stained eyes. A tiny defenseless little child with a small face was restlessly resting in a white blanket. The baby, fit on two palms, seemed so native, so close...

"How many times have I thought that I will never see your angelic face, how many times did I say goodbye to you when you were still in your mother's womb. How many times I bequeathed you to your mother, remaining after me," he thought carefully cuddling her swaddled body.

He touched his wife"s forehead with his lips and handed her a bouquet.

Here people in white coats began to exchange views on how best to name the child.

When the child was still in the womb, Zhanibek said several times that if a girl will be born, he wants to call her "Marua," a name similar to that of her mother. However, probably, fate was so pleasing, her birth turned out to be connected with a lot of events. He seemed to be beyond the veil. And when he said aloud that he would like to name the girl *Makhabbat* in honor of cardiac surgeon Makhabbat Sansyzbaikyzy Bekbossynova, who saved his life, made his heart beat, his wife and all people in white coats joyfully supported him.

So, an infant in honor of woman with golden hands and with a pure heart, cardiologist Bekbossynova began to wear the beautiful name Makhabbat. The father and mother wanted her to become the same wonderful person.

- "As an evidence that the surgery made to you was God's blessing, little Makhabbat had a birthmark right above her heart. Why wasn't it located on the leg, arm, head or other part of the body, right on the chest at the heart? She is like an angel who stood up for her father's life!" – said Munira in three days, having noticed this amazing sky-sign.

Seeing this brown speck on the child's chest, Makhabbat Sansyzbaikyzy was also very surprised, and exclaimed in astonishment:

- "The power of Allah is infinite! The power of Allah is unlimited!"

VII

- "Accept every new day as a gift from the Most High! Be glad to every day! "– advised to Zhanibek Alexander Sazhin, the first Kazakhstani recipient, resident of Kokshetau, who replaced his heart abroad.

Makhabbat Sansyzbaikyzy introduced them in the center, so that he could see with his own eyes how a person with a stranger's heart lives in good health.

Alexander's heart was transplanted in Belarus. It turns out that he doesn't go far for examination, which is supposed to be held quarterly, he passes it here at the Astana National Scientific and Cardiological Center.

- "Our domestic medicine is in no way inferior to Belarusian, so I come here. In Belarus, transplantation issues began to be dealt with in the 70s. Ninety percent of the operated are alive and well to this day. Only in the last three years about thirty patients were operated on. One of them is me. I was brought to Minsk on a stretcher and operated in their Republican Scientific and Practical Center. Everything went well, I returned home on my own feet. In Belarus to find a donor is the main problem. Patients are waiting for organs for transplant in the center for months. How much did you wait for the heart?" - he asked.

- "It was as is a proverb: at the right time in the right place. I came seriously ill and heart was found right away, "- Zhanibek said.

- "You are a lucky guy! And I was lying in a foreign country for almost six months, stupidly and hopelessly waiting for who would die, and if died, whether they will give the heart to me. So it goes, I wanted to live... For these six months I was three times in a state of clinical death. If you knew how much strength is needed to survive on the verge of life and death, wait for a miracle from the Creator! Exhausting fatigue comes, nervous system breaks down."

"And how many young people were then close to me in a state, as they say, one leg here, the other – there. That year I turned forty years old. How many times have I seen how a man with whom I repeatedly communicated, once, lying on his back on a rattling cart, was covered with a white sheet, taken from the ward. There is no guarantee that you will be on this trolley one day. And sometimes, when we find out that one of our recipients had a donor, everyone congratulated him, tore a button off his clothes or begged for something for luck. If a healthy man saw, how we envied, when a person was taken to a surgery, I think he would then understand the dignity of life, the price of health. Of course, we wished the recipient to recover, but with envious thoughts: will such a day come for us, will we be able to once again exit from clinical death. On one of the days between hope and envy, my attending physician reported the glad tidings: there was a heart for me. The seventeen-year-old boy crashed on a motorcycle. With the permission of his parents, his heart was transplanted to me. My heart is only eighteen years old," - said Alexander, and gently tapped his fist onto the heart. He sounded proud.

- "I have to live a long life for myself and for that young man. His parents gave permission for a transplant to keep his son's heart alive. And whose heart do you have?" - he asked.

- "I have a woman's heart ..."

- "Did she have any children?"

-"Of course, two children were left."

- "So, she left without reaching her cherished dream. For these guys, you will be a living witness to the beating of their mother's heart. Therefore, you must live a responsible, long and active life."

- "May it be so! Let me take something from you for luck, and I'll be lucky too, "- Zhanibek laughed.

- "My heart is still not one year old, anyway I will give you this change for luck," - he said, pulled out of his pocket and poured a handful of coins worth 50 and 20 tenge into the palm of Zhanibek.

A good-natured, funny storyteller.

- "Zhanibek, don't be afraid, earlier people with transplanted hearts lived only several months. Then they lived for several years. Today, thanks to new advances in surgical technology, such a surgery extends human life on average by 5-10 years. My son found information on the Internet that in the UK a man, whose name is John McCafferty has been living for more than 30 years with a donor heart. Now he is 70 years old. He leads an active life – swimming, jogging. Waking up every morning he thanks fate for one more lived day. Let's learn from him, my friend. This person is proof that one can live a long life with a heart transplant. We'll celebrate more than one anniversary together," - Alexander Sazhin said to his fate-mate, embracing Zhanibek at partying.

Now Zhanibek is already slowly emerging into the corridors of the center, walking slowly. Reminds him of the child, proud of his first steps. He is proud not only himself, Zhanibek admires all the doctors and nurses of the center, even the technicians and guards standing in the doorway. As soon as he passed them by his uncertain gait, they immediately began to tell each other all the news about the achievements of domestic medicine. 'Here is the result of these achievements,' they said, pointing to Zhanibek. Everyone was pleased with these achievements of Kazakhstani medicine.

The exciting moment in his life was his acquaintance with donor Galina's son Igor Vorotnikov. That morning, Zhanibek, as usual, took medical procedures, was already going out to the corridor to take a walk. Then Makhabbat Sansyzbaikyzy came up to him, smiling with her eyes. In such cases she reported good news. So, with a smile she approached the patient when he had good analysis results.

- "Zhanibek, I'll introduce you to Igor Vorotnikov today," - she said.

At the word "Vorotnikov," Zhanibek's heart began to beat violently. Blood hit his head. Last name of the woman whose heart beats in his chest is Vorotnikova. He also remembers that her son and daughter were left. This is the Igor who, having shown humanity, gave him the heart of his mother. Only God knows, would Zhanibek be alive or not today, if he wouldn't have agreed? Could he see the angelic face of little daughter Makhabbat or not?

In his heart, Zhanibek expected: sooner or later such a meeting will take place. '*How will my heart react when it sees her son, won't it beat so hard thus breaking rhythm of function?!*' – he was afraid of this meeting. And now this moment has come!

Overflowing with feelings, Zhanibek went and sat on the bed. In a while Makhabbat Sansyzbaikyzy returned with a young boy who wore shoe covers on the feet, dressed in a robe, white cap on the head, from under the mask only his eyes shone. The rays stream from the deep blue eyes. Zhanibek didn't see any other parts of the body, he glared at those eyes, his entire inner world shook, his heart rolled to his throat and he didn't notice how he jumped out of bed. Getting up, swayed. Noticing this, the doctor came running up to him.

- "Zhanibek, sit down or you'll fall, "- she said, pressing on his shoulders.

Igor was in great confusion as well.

The heart of his mother, his beloved mother, was beating in the chest of this man!

More than a month has passed since the death of his mother, but her sweet heart, MOM'S HEART, which he and his sister Veronica loved, is on Earth!

This heart will still live among people, function. Now this heart pulsates in Zhanibek's chest, still good continues to love people.

Galina Konstantinovna really was a very merciful person!

She loved her students, respected their parents, shared with them all that she knew. She was a teacher, whom countrymen were proud of. She loved her Motherland Kazakhstan! To the questions consanguines from other countries "How did you get there?", she would proudly answer "We were born there. This is our Homeland." And she would say to her children, "Kazakhstan is your Homeland. Never even think about moving to another country. Kazakhs are your brothers. We will not assimilate into another place." She would repeat that often, as if feeling early departure from life. This amazing and wide heart, like the Kazakh steppe, of a Russian woman was now beating in the chest of her Kazakh brother.

Igor speechless rushed to Zhanibek's chest, in which his mother's heart was beating. Two embraces closed.

The mother's heart was beating between the two guys!

Hot tears streamed from Igor's eyes and were absorbed into the mask fabric. Zhanibek's tears also streamed down onto the medical face mask...

No words were needed to describe this amazing meeting. The hearts understood each other without words, the souls were excited, and the blood was pounding in their veins...

Makhabbat Sansyzbaikyzy eyes were wet, silently watching this scene of their meeting. She stroked the guys on the head with her thin beautiful fingers and asked them to calm down. One sat on the bed, and the other on a chair.

Igor was unable to say anything. Zhanibek was silent too, silently looking down, as if listening to something.

Makhabbat Sansyzbaikyzy told the men a little about the history of the surgery and left, taking Igor with her.

Zhanibek is still unable to recover.

The poor heart felt that the guy was part of it. He was excited, a lump rolled up to throat, he wanted to cry as if he wanted to leave with Igor...

He wanted to lie down, but it did not work.

That night he did not fall asleep. Igor's eyes were standing before his eyes. The Mother's Heart plunged him into a state of anxiety for her son...

VIII

On August 29, Makhabbat Sansyzbaikyzy, Zhanibek and Igor invited Eugeny Kurtz, whose kidney was replaced, together with the freelance transplant from the Ministry of Health Gani Kuttymuratov, they held a press conference at the Center for representatives of the domestic media.

Representatives of the media who heard about the first heart replacement surgery in our country , which was held twenty days ago, but did not know the details, filled the small hall of the Center. Such an event was not a curiosity for doctors, but Zhanibek and Igor were hardly breathing, blood was pounding in temples, and they felt giddy from the numerous eyes looking at them. Flicking of shutters and flashes of cameras, chirrups of TV cameras blinded them, did not allow them to concentrate. Zhanibek felt restrained by breathing, it became difficult to breathe under the mask. The heart, not yet accustomed to the new body, was beating faster, as if it wanted to jump out of the throat. But he tried not to give a look. In the beginning, two doctors in detail told the audience the whole history of this event. Then the questions of journalists showered. They, of course, were primarily interested in the state of health of Eugene and Zhanibek. Igor Vorotnikov remained under the hail of questions. Some praised his civil feat and noble deed, which had not before been done by anyone in our country, others admired others, others simply marveled. Igor, who kept himself judicious and thoughtful, found the answers to all questions. This very young man spoke weighty, meaningful words, calmly treated some, sometimes even not entirely correct, questions about the organs of the mother.

Completely exhausted from the meeting, which lasted one hour, Zhanibek hardly got to the ward...

Information from this press conference was transmitted after lunch on the same day, it did not cease to spread for three days, reached the remotest corners of the republic, was replicated in the CIS countries. ULT portal – the socio-political online publication, among the media, they covered this main event in the clearest way. The article of journalist Saken Abdiyev "Death. Decision. Life." with pictures of Zhanibek, Eugene and Igor, made a special impression on the doctors and characters themselves. We offer some information without change to the attention of the readers of this book.

Death. Decision. Life.

Yesterday transplantologists of Kazakhstan announced their achievements. The patient, who in the Center of Cardiac Surgery of Astana for the first time in our country was transplanted donor heart, and the young man who gave him the heart of his mother, appeared in front of journalists.

Igor Vorotnikov is a simple man who has nothing to do with medicine. But this person will remain in the history of medicine in Kazakhstan, writes <u>*Bnews*</u>*. The boy who lost his mother made two families happy.*

Mother's heart

About a month ago, Igor allowed to be transplanted the heart and kidney of his mother, who died of a stroke – a hemorrhage in the brain, to two citizens who needed these organs. In the Astana Cardiosurgical Center, together with Zhanibek Ospanov, in whose chest his mother's heart beats, and Eugeny Kurtz, to whom his mother's kidneys saved life, hiding tears in his eyes and restraining pain in his heart, held an open press conference for journalists.

On August 6, 2012 in Astana, a 46-year-old woman was taken to the hospital with brain hemorrhage. Speaking in the language of medicine, she was a "dead person." However, her heart continued to beat evenly. At this time countryman of Galina Vorotnikova, 38-year-old resident of Rudny Zhanibek Ospanov, needed an urgent heart replacement surgery. In the world practice of organ transplantation there are certain established methods. If someone suddenly dies, with the consent of relatives, you can give life to another person. A person taking a foreign organ is called a recipient, and a giver is called a donor.

The Astana surgeons did not hesitate. Immediately took urgent measures. First of all, they notified the son of the dying woman, Igor Vorotnikov.

"I was informed about the death of my mother's brain and was told that her active heart can be transplanted to another person. I thought that her life could be saved by connecting to a device. It turns out that we don't have such a device. I thought for a long time. Then I was allowed to examine her body. I kept thinking about my mother. When I saw that person, his family, I realized that my mother would not mind such a decision. If my mother were at that moment able to answer the questions, I think she would support my decision," Igor said.

Domestic clinics earlier performed other organ transplantation. However, the heart was transplanted for the first time. Responsible surgery was conducted on August 8.

A vital decision

Igor Vorotnikov made an important decision in his life. Two families depended on his and his little sisters decision. After much thought, Igor agreed to transfer his mother's heart to Zhanibek Ospanov, and the kidneys to another recipient Eugeny Kurtz. Both surgeries were successful. Doctors of the National Scientific Cardiosurgery Center reported that both patients who had heart and kidney transplants felt well. In the near future they will go home.

"Now, looking at Zhanibek, I know that my mother's heart continues

to beat. Yesterday night the wife of the man whom my mother's heart gave life, gave birth to his daughter. The person with the heart of my mother will raise a future "mother," Igor said.

During the press conference, all doctors expressed admiration for Igor's noble deed. Many, perhaps, simply can not understand what a vital decision he made. However, this was the decision that changed the lives of others."

Let's dwell on the feedback of readers at the bottom of this article:

Indira: The man who lost his mother, but managed to give life to others, I can't say anything except for gratitude...

Zhomart: Dear Igor, I wish you and your little sister happiness! You are a man with a big heart. Such people should always be helped everywhere.

Yergaly Baizak: Not all of us is capable of this. Well done, IGOR!!!" he expresses his gratitude.

And next to it there is another opinion:

"???: I would not give consent to such a donation. How can you allow dismemberment of your mother, incomprehensible, the soul shudders? The way a person came to this world, so he must leave it. Isn't it so?" one of our compatriots wrote.

As is known, there are a lot of people who agree with the latter opinion, opponents of the removal of organs of the deceased. Especially a lot of those who resist this, referring to the Sharia. Were their opinions considered, but the article "Is it possible to transplant the organ (transplantation)?" is posted on the Agmeshit.kz website. Without changing anything, I offer it to your opinion.

"In some cases, the prohibitions indicated in the Shariah can be changed in cases of extreme necessity.

For example, when a pregnant woman dies, her live fetus is extracted by cutting her stomach. Although the mother is dead, the baby needs to be saved, he must live. (Ikhtiyar, 4:167; Raddul Mukhtar, 1:602) Based on this provision, Muslim theologians also permit replacement of organs of the body. In such cases, heart, kidneys, eyes and other organs of deceased person are seized.

This is what Ahmad ash-Shirbasi, a scientist at the world university of al-Azhar in Cairo, says about this, "Before such a surgery, it is necessary to take into account some circumstances. The organ must be replaced only to a person who is on the verge of life and death.

Along with this, the decision on the surgery must be made and taken by a person who is versed in these matters. Not every doctor can do this. Besides, there must be a document on the consent of the deceased about the seizure of his organ. In the absence of such a paper, there must be consent of the deceased's relatives. And if the deceased in his lifetime bequeathed "after my death, do not touch my body," then no one has the right to extract his organs. Body organ is extracted only from the deceased person. The living is not seized. The organ is not taken even from a person who is in the state of death. Since there are many cases when a person whom doctors consider hopeless, by the will of Allah returns to life.

Therefore, considering "he will still die" it is not allowed by our faith to remove the organ from a dying person and transplant it to another. Sometimes a living person gives one kidney to a dying person. In this case, this can be allowed if it does not harm the surrendering person. Since the goal is to save a person's life, giving an organ is allowed only in case of emergency.

The Quran states: **"If anyone kills an innocent person, this is equated with the murder of all mankind. And the salvation of one person is equated to the salvation of all mankind."** *(Maida, 32 Ayat). Relying on this postulate, scientists only allow the giving of blood to a bloodless person. It is allowed even to take blood from a non-Muslim person (Yasalunaka fid-din ul-hayat, 1:604-608). A person who has given his organ to another does not have to charge for it. The human body is not a commodity that can be traded in a store or in a market," the scientist said.*

Reading the last sentence of this article, I want to remind again that Igor Vorotnikov, giving his mother's internal organs, pursued a good goal – that compatriots needing them could live. The Russian man, after giving the organs of his mother's body to Kazakh and German, didn't demand money from them.

The help was provided from purely humane motives!

In recent years, offers like "selling a kidney, I'll share a liver" and others were advertised. During the study of the surgery history of Zhanibek, I saw an article written by a colleague Serikhan Khasen, which was called "Tortures of replacement of a human organ." After reading it, I was amazed. I want to tell the general content of the article to the readers of this story.

"This was in the spring of this year. I was on the bus. A man of about thirty sat on the next seat. He was talkative, so we got aquainted. He said he works at the construction site. I answered that I am a correspondent of a newspaper. He immediately became attached: "If you're a journalist, help me write an announcement about the sale of the kidney to close the loan. Only one request: don't write my real name, it is inconvenient for acquaintances and relatives."

"Actually, our newspaper doesn't publish ads. There are special editions for this," I was embarrassed. "Then talk to them." Since I had never heard of sale of kidneys before I was a bit confused, didn't know how to continue the conversation.

He continued, "This year I'll be thirty-two years old. I have a professional education. I am the father of three children. I don't suffer from any diseases (tapped his muscular arm on the chest). Just problems above the throat. Full blast of debts: to the bank and people. This, bro, is the only way to pay off with everyone. Maybe there are people who need kidneys. Will you help me?" he asked and looked inquiringly into my face. "What about you?" "What me? People live with one kidney, I won't die. Just need to get rid of this misfortune" (he probably meant debts). "Understand me and my wife are unemployed. Who will pay the debts, if not me? I'd rather die with honor and without debts!"

Apparently, the voice of my interlocutor sounded louder, people began to turn around. "Think again. Maybe there are other ways to solve the problem," I said not letting him go.

"How much I can think. With my salary in this world, I will hardly pay off with debts. Instead of decreasing, they grow. I don't want my children to know about the unhappy situation. You know, I don't event want to live. There is no worse humiliation when you don't have an opportunity to help distressed relatives!"

"Does your wife know about this decision?" I asked. "She doesn't, I don't want her to know. That's why I'm want the add is with a different name."

I continues to ask, "Where did you get this idea?" "I heard on TV. A guy told how he sold his kidney for 10 thousand USD and it dawned on me," he smiled.

"Won't it turn out that grief will add to your debts, you'll be suffering with one kidney?" I involuntarily exclaimed.

"And what to do – there is no other way out. Let it be what it should be..." he answered. He couldn't hide the wrinkles on his forehead and the burst of sorrow.

"How did you end up in the grip of such debts?" I asked, wanting to get him to talk. "I took the first debt when my daughter went to paid school. Although the salary was small, they somehow gave the loan. Then the son went to paid school. And for him I took a debt. Then my father died. Where to go – again to the bank. So gradually, imperceptibly plunged into the quagmire of debts. Loans were not closed on time, then interest grew. That's how I was imprisoned in this trouble," the helpless adult man concluded grievously.

"I am the youngest in the family, the only son. The elder sisters are all married. After the death of father, I took the mother, who lived in the village, to live with us place. This is my situation," he concluded his sad story.

He turned out already missed his stop. He left his phonenumber. Leaving the bus he said, "Buddy, call me for sure" and waved to me...

Here is quite an opposite story.

Ularbek (name changed) is looking for a kidney. He says he's ready to pay 5 thousand USD to a person who will give him the kidney. However, still no one wants to sell him a kidney. Reason is that the kidney is actually worth five times more . Ularbek is also an Almaty man. He has been suffering from illness for three years already. The doctors said that both kidneys are unwell. He would like to "update" at least one kidney. Now three times a week he goes to one of their clinical hospitals in the city and takes treatment.

"Previously, I worked as a cash courier. In 2007 I got ill. The diagnosis was pyelonephritis. First, only the lower back seemed to ache. Later it was clear that my kidneys got out of order. I passed treatment in various hospitals, was in the Syzganov center. They cleaned my blood there. As I was told, food gets into the blood, due to inaction or poor performance of the kidneys, the blood begins to deteriorate. In the Syzganov center they took out harmful substances from the blood, I felt that the kidneys improved. However, the doctors said to replace the kidneys you need to find a donor. Once the kidneys can generally refuse to function. Now I am an invalid of the second category. The state pays me benefits," he complained about his helpless condition.

Recently I heard such unpleasant news. A girl-first-grader disappeared in one of the villages near Almaty. Her parents were looking for her everywhere. Reported to the law enforcement agencies. They couldn't find the child. She was found in three days – someone brought her to the house yard. The child was unconscious. They urgently took her to the hospital, it turned out that one of her kidneys was cut out...

Judging by such reports, trafficking in human beings, or rather, trafficking in organs of the human body, is now in full swing. The reason is simple: now people who need transplant of kidney, liver, heart, pancreas, are so many that they cannot be counted. Countless people need to replace organs.

Such surgeries in our country are done at the A.N.Syzganov National Scientific and Surgical Center (Almaty) and at the Republican Scientific Center of Emergency Medical Assistance (Astana). In the centers, the replacement of organs is carried out by highly qualified specialists. To be more precise, up to 10 doctors participate in one surgery. The centers are not limited to the replacement of kidneys and liver, and in accordance with the requirements of modern medicine transplanted the heart, lungs, liver and pancreas.

Among organ replacements, the heart replacement is the most dangerous. If you look at the statistics, in the world, ten people in every million people need a transplant. On the complexity of the surgery, the second place is taken by kidney transplantation. 90 percent of the patients operated on the kidneys survive. There are many people in the country with viral, autoimmune and toxic kidney lesions. By the degree of complexity, the third place is occupied by transplantation of the pancreas. The pancreas is the organ that restores the degree of glycemia in diabetic patients. Therefore, as claimed, damage to the pancreas is fraught with big troubles.

Just look around – everything is sold!

We thought that only a' person' is not sold. Now he is sold too. If earlier western spare parts for the car were sold, now more and more often spare parts (organs) of people are exhibited on an open sale. From year to year the number of people selling and acquiring human organs increases. Experts say that any organ other than the brain can be transplanted. The heart, liver (part), kidneys, seminal cells, eyes, even the spinal cord (part) are exposed to trade. Information about all this can be found on the Internet.

Reading the ads of people who want to sell organs, you are convinced that many are going to this because of the deteriorating living conditions. And according to experts, in the future such "donors" expect a hard life. One example: people who gave a kidney are more likely to be exposed to viral infections. They cannot do hard work. Should eat little salt food.

Currently, replacement of organs in the world is carried out according to two legal norms. According to the rules established by the World Health Organization, it is allowed to be a donor by agreement or presumption of consent (after the death of a person, his organs can be withdrawn only with the consent of relatives). In such a situation, after death of a person, heart should be set to another person within 4 hours, the liver – 6-8 hours. Therefore, a person who needs such organs, should conclude an agreement with the relatives of the dying person in advance. This type of transplantation is now often carried out in Spain, Austria and Belgium. In these countries, a single deceased brings income up to 250 thousand USD. Transplantation by permission of the donor is mainly carried out in the USA, Great Britain and Holland. In Kazakhstan, the number of people who need organ replacement exceeds 4000 people, including heart-1200, liver-1200, kidney-2000.

In such a situation, I think it would be inappropriate to talk about whether Igor acted right or wrong, giving his mother's organs to two citizens for free, and thereby saved their lives. It remains only to thank Igor Vorotnikov.

In such a situation, the lines of the poem of great Kazakh poet Mukagali Makatayev pop up in memory, during whose life transplantation was not among the discussed problems, it was not even talked about in society. Here they are:

"I am a donor.
I have beneficial blood.
Take it, take it.
Learn property of
My warm blood.
No!
I will not sell for money!
I give my debts
To all the sick.
Giving life to another,
I keep my own!"

(interlinear translation)

Although it is only about giving blood, the deepest thought is the salvation of man. "Whoever gave the blood, he gave the soul," our ancestors said. And how to name the one who gave the person the only heart of his Mother?!

Anyway, what could be better than when, if possible, you stand up for a person's life, not for money, but for conscience, you fulfill your duty to extend, even for one day, the happiness of seeing this world.

IX

Twenty-three days passed after the surgery, and it was decided to discharge Zhanibek from the hospital. Now he will plunge into the thickness of other people of Astana and will deal with everyday affairs. Until now, he came from Kostanay for medical treatment, but did not inspect Astana purposefully, did not stay here. Now, he has to become a resident of this city for some time. He needs to come to the Center twice a week to take tests. And for this it is necessary for himself, his wife and daughter to rent a suitable apartment. Until the heart finally becomes accustomed to his nature, the blood will not circulate normally in the body, he should not move away from the treating doctors.

Women, as always, are practical. Munira, while in the maternity home, taking care of the child, managed to find an apartment for rent in the newspaper "Over-the-counter." The rent was requested, not much, not less, 130 thousand tenge per month. Where could the sick and treated young family find such money? Makhabbat Sansyzbaikyzy came to the help again. At her insistence, the cardiosurgical center staff managed to find a sponsor and pay for the apartment. For three months he lived in this apartment, twice a week carefully passed tests.

Zhanibek became a member of the Republican public association "Nurly Kogam," organized by patients who need organ and tissue transplantation. He shared with his brothers in misfortune with the history of his illness and cure.

The man is happy with the fact, how his body gets stronger every day, the desire for life grows. Holding the small daughter in his arms, he listens with pleasure to her buzzing and the soul is filled with happiness. There is nothing strange in the body, worrying him. Feels, if he really can turn mountains. Climbing the stairs, he counts the steps, trains, gradually increasing their number. He walks by himself to the store and the pharmacy, located near the house. And when Munira leaves on some business, he stays with small Makhabbat. Sometimes he goes out for a walk with her.

Going outside he doesn't forget to wear a mask. Carefully observes the regimens for taking medications, takes food strictly on a diet, doesn't eat after 6 p.m. The love of meat is inherent in blood of our people, but Zhanibek eats very little. His main dishes are vegetables and fruits, milk and ayran. Munira is on maternity leave, and his disability pension is poor. However, they learned to be content with little, he is happy that his wife and child are alive and close.

He left the house five months ago, now, with an improvement in his health, he was relentlessly dragged to his native land, living in one room became a burden, he was bored and more and more often began to think about Kostanay.

- "No, Zhan, you cannot. You just began to come to senses, you can pick up some infection. Be content with this day. I'd better invite relatives here one by one," - Munir retorted against his departure home.

- "Why bother them, I'll be wearing a mask and nothing will happen to me, "- he resented childishly.

He called to Kokshetau friend on the common fate Alexander Sazhin, consulted with him on what transport to go home. He said, "By air it is better than by train, you will quickly reach, and there will be less risk of catching something. If only the heart can stand." "My health now, like a good horse, my heart has grown in me as if I was born with me," Zhanibek assured his friend.

He angrily protested everyone who said that the take-off and landing of the aircraft will heavily influence on the heart:

- "Why don't you believe me, I feel fine?!"

He insistedly repeated to Makhabbat Sansyzbaikzyzy about his excellent health. Finally, a week before the New Year, he got her permission.

The longing for the house won. He flew on an airplane in a literal and figurative sense, like on wings. He didn't take off the mask, tried to sit in the cabin farther from other passengers. After 1 hour 20 minutes he was on native land. He felt like was born again after the surgery. He felt himself a new, finally recovered, Zhanibek. He inhales the air, walks on his native land, which he didn't think he would see. The heart beat violently, alump rolled to the throat. But it was not the same morbid state of the body, but a manifestation of joy.

These were powerful blows of the heart, striving for a new life!

From the excitement, pressure increased a little , but in general, Zhanibek, a cheerful forty-year-old jigit at the airport, got into the car and drove to Rudny.

From the very first days of her stay in Rudny, Munira was making all the visitors wear masks, looked severely if someone coughed or sneezed. She remembered Makhabbat Sansyzbaikyzy's strict instructions that "we should not reduce the level of work of the immune system." She was carrying a stethoscope and medicines always. Fussed with Zhanibek more than with a baby, looked into his mouth, God forbid, eating fatty meat, juicy kazy and karta. Being among his relatives, Zhanibek felt freer, more confident. If Munira does not remind him – he could forget to take medicine.

Seeing the already strengthened Zhanibek, his shining eyes, listening to his cheerful speeches, the relatives were sincerely happy and thanked the doctors, praised Allah, by whose benevolence all this happened. But some considered Munira's custody of her husband superfluous, limiting his will. *Slaps on his wrists, watches his mouth, doesn't let him do anything on his own,* they muttered, dissatisfied with behavior of the daughter-in-law. Six days passed among relatives in the twinkling of an eye.

The morning of December 31, 2013 came, the year of Serpent was knocking on the door. Munira covered a plentiful dastarkhan, alternately accepted the friends and relatives of Zhanibek.

Zhanibek felt himself again born into this world, to begin a new life. Warmly and cordially he greeted relatives and friends, altogether on the phone congratulated common acquaintances.

Congratulated Igor Vorotnikov and his sister Veronika on the New Year, thanks to whom he lived to this day. They said that they missed their mother, the three of them talked in a relative way, weighed down.

Of course, he did not forget to congratulate noble people in white coats dear to his heart. Is there enough words and feelings to express all the gratitude to Yuri Vladimirovich and Makhabbat Sansyzbaikyzy!

The clock struck midnight. On the national television channel, the New Year's greetings of President of the Republic of Kazakhstan Nursultan Nazarbayev started. Listening to the congratulation of Yelbasy with a tiny child on his knees and in an embrace with his wife, Zhanibek entered a new life...

The exhausting long winter of Sary-Arka is behind. Bright March morning, rejoicing in the warm sunshine, cheerfully and confidently treading on his native land, Zhanibek went to work.

A little away from home, he looked back.

His wife and daughter waved at him from the window. Happy from what he saw, he waved back and walked on.

A long life full of deep meaning, great happiness and hard work is ahead...

X

In the sixth operating room
2013. August.

The media of the country vied with each other to inform that the year has passed since the heart transplant surgery was performed for the first time at the National Scientific and Cardiological Center of Kazakhstan, located in Astana. The media reported: a man with a new heart, Zhanibek Ospanov started to work along with all citizens with full health serves the Homeland, feeds his family.

I came to a meeting with the Center management with my finished story about this historical event. A Korean by nationality, Yuri Vladimirovich, telling me that he likes to be called "the swarthy son of the Kazakh people," and that he understands the Kazakh language pretty well, greeted me in Kazakh.

He asked to leave my composition, when he read it with cardiac surgeon Saltanat Abdizhanapkyzy Andossova, he got her opinion and invited me to the center. With his permission I got acquainted with today's life of the Center.

Most importantly, I took part in a surgery performed by this cardiac surgeon with golden hands, and she made an indelible impression on me. Such happiness, such luck doesn't fall on every journalist and writer. Therefore I decided to complete my narrative by describing it.

Yuri Vladimirovich instructed Saltanat Abdizhanapkyzy to show me all operating rooms, to tell about the work of this very respectable institution.

So, we pass the operational block of the Center.

The center consists of three branches with six operating rooms. Each department has two operating rooms. Ten surgeries are held daily, they work continuously. Two operating rooms are for children.

In the operating room, where we entered at the very beginning, we were met by the smell of burnt skin. I involuntarily winced at the unpleasant smell. Noticing this, Saltanat warned me:

- "This smell of burnt skin appears at the opening of the chest cavity. If you feel bad because of the smell, and you'll also see blood, you may feel dizzy, say about it right away. Not all ordinary people properly perceive this."

The smell, of course, was unpleasant for me, but I decided to endure everything to the end and asked to continue the tour.

Intubation – preparation for surgery – is performed here. Anesthesiologist Myrzabek Makhmutov, being at his workplace, explained the essence of held measures.

In the next surgery room, expert Lyazzat Sagadatkyzy, putting a thin tube through the mouth of a patient, observes the heart by echocardiography. Here I was given an explanation by cardiac surgeon Yermagambet Kuatbayev:

- "We used to treat heart failure only with medicines before. New methods of treatment opened in national medicine. At intervention devices that give the heart additional impulses are set. An additional heart is connected. There is an opportunity to replace the third heart, thanks to this the patient returned to life.

Last year's heart replacement surgery of Ospanov was the first achievement along this way. It was effective, the patient is now among healthful people, already working. It is only necessary that he regularly takes prescribed medications, and he will not be worse than his peers..."

In the next room, a female surgeon held a surgery. In the surgical attire, only the eyes of a tall, fragile woman, are visible. It turns out that this profession, which requires courage and intelligence, and sometimes-physical strength, representatives of the fair sex have started to master.

- "We have more girls-surgeons – Sveta, Aray, Schnar, Zhanna and Assel. They hold surgeries no worse than men, their hands are strong, "- Saltanat Abdizhanapkyzy praised her colleagues.

Here, anesthesiologist Daniyar Abishev gave anesthesia to the patient, who was going for shunting.

And I hurried to get to the sixth operating room, where the gold hand of Kazakhstan surgery Yuri Vladimirovich Pya operated on that day.

At the entrance to the operating room in a green surgical suit, in the optical glasses, "swarthy son of the Kazakh people" of medium height, cardiac surgeon Yuri Vladimirovich washed his hands. He has made more than ten thousand successful surgeries. Rolling up his sleeves to his elbows he carefully soaped his hands, rubbing every finger. In the meantime, he consulted about something with the department head who had entered. Then, from the tap of the container hanging on the wall he rinsed his hands with an antiseptic and headed to the hall. The sliding door opened noiselessly. Immediately the equipment, which even for an uninitiated person was evidently the most modern, corresponding to the world standards, caught the eye.

In the room, which four walls are sheathed with steel, upon entering a person's face is hit with cold. Two six-lobed operating lamps hang from the ceiling.

An operating table is in the middle of the room. A monitor is set at the head board.

In the back of the room there is a minilab.

On one side, the pacemaker controls the heart rhythm.

The entire work of the surgeon can be observed on the monitor, hanging from the left side of the operating table.

In the room, given the complexity of the surgery, there are two cardiosurgeons, one perfusionist, one anesiologist and their assistants.

The anesthetist put a robe on Yuri Vladimirovich. Tying the belt, he came up to the operating table. Robes, gloves, other things and tools in open-heart surgery are used only once.

This surgery – mamor-coronary bypass surgery – was to be done to a young man from Kyrgyzstan, who heard about the fame of cardiac surgeon Pya. The surgery is performed with an active heart. Such a surgery in the world is done only by cardiac surgeons of the highest category. Surgery with an active heart does not harm the brain. The physiological state of a person is preserved. Blood does not liquefy, the kidneys do not experience over load. The minimum amount of medicine is used. And if you do surgery with a stopped heart, at reconnection, the human body is experiencing great difficulties.

The surgeon picked up the electric saw and began to cut his chest. Cutting 25 centimeters, he stopped. The smell of burnt skin spread across the room.

The human meat, devoid of blood, turns out to be slightly yellow and resembles meat from the refrigerator.

In the open chest cavity, I saw a real beating heart...

Yuri Vladimirovich cauterized small blood vessels in the cuts by coagulator, reminiscent of a pen. There are thousands of such vessels, cauterization is not dangerous. Large blood vessels are dangerous, they are stitched.

In one hand Yuri Vladimirovich holds forceps tweezer made of a special alloy, in the other hand – an electroscalpel. There are no old metal ones now... There are two buttons that are pressed in turn on the electroscalpel. No one tells the surgeon which and when to press them, he feels it intuitively, depending on experience and skill.

The operating table is able to rotate, move in different directions. The surgeon can, if necessary, perform the surgery sitting.

On the other side of the table, the student of Pya Darhan retrieves a blood vessel from the patient's leg. Having prepared everything, he approached the mentor and began to help him.

It turns out there are many preparations used in post-operative cardiac start – milrinone, dobutamine and other medications that don't allow for lowering of blood pressure, lulling, not affecting negatively on the brain.

The day before the surgery, the patient undergoes a comprehensive examination, in the blood department about ten people prepare the necessary blood. If the patient loses blood during the surgery, they immediately come to the rescue. On the one hand, blood is poured in, on the other – a minilab works. No lab technician is needed here. Special devices under constant control keep the presence of oxygen, hydrocarbon and hemoglobin.

"When you'll be abroad, you will see the same, we have even better than in some countries. Even the walls are special here. When the building was under construction, Yuri Vladimirovich was constantly here, kept everything under control himself: implemented, installed everything he saw in Europe, explained everyone what the operating unit should be like. These lamps perform many functions, they even have cameras, they film the course of the surgery. Previously, for training purposes, the interns had to drop in and look from behind the surgeon's back. Lamps are multifunctional: they record and demonstrate in a large hall through a monitor. Besides, from here on the microphone you can communicate with a large hall. Sometimes they ask questions. Surgeons and cardiologists who come to Kazakhstan from anywhere for rare and complex surgeries communicate directly with the operating unit, ask questions and get answers," Saltanat Abdizhanapkyzy explained to me.

"This man is head of the department Rymbay Kaliuly. He makes constant rounds, watches how many people entered the operating room, how many went out, how many pass. Particular attention is paid to air. Any change in air is dangerous. The main thing here is the preservation of sterility. If you remember, blue lamps were used before, now they are not. Did you notice the movement of cold air? This is called *laminar flow*. Abroad, the old air is withdrawn, fresh is let in. Everything is completely ventilated, regulated. This is called *aseptic of the highest degree*. The smelling chlorine is not used for weashing, as before. This is also done in our wards, we do nothing else but clean the air.

Yuri Vladimirovich attaches great importance to all this in the Center. "The surgery is a very difficult deed. If a patient dies at the end of the surgery, all the work was in vain, state money will be wasted. Labor of surgeons and cardiologists become useless. Therefore, today, aseptic is in the first place," she continues.

I imagined that in the place where the surgery is performed, blood flows as a river. And here is not a drop of blood. All is sucked off by a small pump, processed and re-infused into the patient. The thread that stitches wounds together are not even seen. They can be seen only in optical glasses, which increase the objects tenfold. It feels like tweezers are moving through the air.

A blood vessel taken from the leg is used for bypass surgery. The place from which it was taken is sewed from two sides. In the future, there will be no harm to leg from this. How clever it was to start using own vessels for better health! However, this surgery must be done correctly. Otherwise, the leg may swell.

One surgery, as a rule, is carried out jointly by four or five branches. Sometimes it happens that the surgery is carried out all night. At the Center, all surgery is 100% covered by state funds. Foreigners pay for themselves. The person who was operated on that day came from Bishkek.

Yuri Vladimirovich worked for several years in Kyrgyzstan. That's why patients come from there. Ten years he worked abroad. After graduation in Moscow because of a lack of a surgeon's job, he worked as a traumatologist. At the first opportunity, he was transferred to cardiosurgery. The center was built under his direct control, now he heads it. Today, international surgeries are being carried out here. Now our patients do not go abroad for heart surgery. The most sick come here.

Yuri Vladimirovich is fond of Eastern philosophy. He shares good thoughts from it with doctors, he speaks not only medical topics on planners, but also raises questions of universal value that affect the consciousness of colleagues. He strives to improve their level of development not only on a professional level. He never tires of repeating to his students "Not a single moment should be wasted. Thoughts that come to mind today, tomorrow may not visit you. It is necessary to do today. It is necessary to use every second. Do not get tired. A person who wants to master his work must come to work at six in the morning and leave at ten. There are all conditions for learning. Don't be lazy!"

He helps everyone who has the ability and wants to work. Today, his inmates work in all regions of Kazakhstan. If necessary, he can fly to any of them to help. He mastered English and Turkish languages. He seeks to introduce in Kazakhstan any medical novelty, which has appeared in the world. Last year, when the congress of cardiosurgeons was held, dozens of foreign medical scientists were invited and participated at his initiative.

According to colleagues, 55-year-old Yuri Vladimirovich is terse, never raises his voice, is very simple in communication. Equally welcoming to both the child and the elderly person. There were cases when he conducted surgeries for 6-10 hours in a row. He knows arrhythmology well, there's no need to mention cardiology.

In order to become a surgeon, above all, patience is needed. Strong nature and courage are needed. All this is inherent in Mr. Pya. In the world surgeons are divided into adult surgeons and surgeons for children. Yuri Vladimirovich is one of the rare surgeons in the world who makes surgeries to both age categories.

There are many legends about Yury Vladimirovich. He above all prises such categories as purity and honesty, firmly adheres to the principle "the doctor must help the enemy too."

This is he who organized planting of bushes near the Center, watches cleanliness as in his own house. Perfect cleanliness and order amaze foreign visitors.

Head of the department Rymbay Kaliuly constantly entered all six operating rooms, learned about their condition and informed everyone. If in one of them a violation was detected, he immediately took up putting it in order. That's how for days he's shuffling among all the halls.

Yuri Vladimirovich is also involved in the training of personnel for the whole of Kazakhstan.

One day, the surgery is done by Pya, on the other – by his student. The heads of the three branches of the Center are his graduates, today each of them is able to independently conduct surgeries. If necessary, they seek advice from their mentor. At monthly reports of the supervisors, the mentor is constantly interested in how many and how the young doctors performed surgeries. He asks why, for what reason, one or another specialist has performed few operations. Never stints on advice.

If a patient's condition worsens after the surgery, all surgeons and cardiologists gather – they are looking for the reasons, find out whether the surgery was correctly performed. After the surgery, Yuri Vladimirovich enters the intensive care unit without fail, checks the patient's condition. Constantly worries until the patient recovers.

The operation in the sixth room also ended successfully.

Thanking head of the department Saltanat Abdizhanapkyzy, who became my guide at the Center for some time, I finish this narrative.

ASTANA, 2013

CONTENTS

Lightning Source UK Ltd.
Milton Keynes UK
UKHW041139171019
351783UK00001B/6/P